Cure

Cure

by **Todd Parnell**
with **Dr. Patrick Parnell**

Acclaim Press
MORLEY, MISSOURI

P.O. Box 238
Morley, MO 63767
(573) 472-9800
www.acclaimpress.com

Book & Cover Design: Frene Melton
Cover art: "Humanity" by Betty Parnell

ISBN: 978-1-948901-93-2 | 1-948901-93-5
Library of Congress Control Number: 2021938791

First Printing: 2021
Printed in the United States of America
10 9 8 7 6 5 4 3 2 1

This publication was produced using available information.
The publisher regrets it cannot assume responsibility for errors or omissions.

DEDICATION

To Betty, of course, whom I have
spent more time with
and grown closer to during this pandemic
than at any time before
in our forty-four years together. . . .

CONTENTS

"The symptoms of love were the same as those of cholera."
Gabriel Garcia Marquez
Love in the Time of Cholera

chapter one

APPLAUSE

THE SETTING SUN SHONE BRIGHTLY ON THE TWO ADULTS SITTING SOCIALLY DISTANCED in the small backyard of Henry Hoary's town house. Heni White sipped from a glass of Butter Chardonnay, Henry a Corona Light. They said nothing, but their eyes locked in a shared gaze spoke more than words.

Heni glanced around and, seeing no one, set her wine on the small table beside her. She rose slowly, unbuttoned her blue blouse, and let it slide into the vacated chair. Next off was the bra revealing small but firm breasts. The fierce sunlight lit up her dark skin.

Henry stared in confusion and wonder. He had never seen anything or one so beautiful. He mumbled something unintelligible.

Heni undid her belt and released her jeans to the ground below, followed by her sheer blue panties. She stepped out of both and slowly covered the distance between her and Henry. She unbuckled his belt, pulled his Levis and boxer shorts down, and mounted him slowly and sensually. Henry could only groan.

It didn't take long for them to near fulfillment as it had been a long time for each between lovers. The shrinking sunlight only fueled their passion. The tried unsuccessfully to swallow moans of pleasure.

Heni collapsed forward on Henry's chest, drawing him close to her. She then leaned in and kissed him deeply.

Somewhere close by they heard applause.

And then a voice shouted out, "Thank you two! We need something to smile about during these crazy times!"

Henry blushed. Heni grinned, before returning to pick up her discarded clothes and motioning for Henry to follow her inside.

"Guess if I've got it, you have it now, too," she purred.

Henry followed her slender figure blindly, wondering to himself if what had just happened was real or just another by-product of an overwrought imagination brought on by the coronavirus crisis at hand.

chapter two

HENI AND HENRY

Heni White was anything but. Her ebony skin was a rich and elegant testimony to her deep African roots. She had no idea where her given surname came from but presumed it had something to do with slavery somewhere in her way back lineage.

Henrietta White was thirty years old, the product of a failed marriage and single mom parenting, who had escaped a like fate by earning scholarships through college and graduate school to become a writer for a major Midwestern magazine in a large metropolitan market. She had been on assignment for several weeks in a small regional office in Southwest Missouri, tracking the spread of the coronavirus pandemic through a region colloquially known as the Mozarks and its seeming success in containing its advancement.

Heni was no virgin but not a sleep-around either. She enjoyed men and their company in general, though pompous, self-inflated rogues really pissed her off. She simply hadn't had time for them in either her studies or her labors.

Of her five or six casual affairs, none had fulfilled her over time. Either the excitement wore off or advanced beyond bearable. All had been with men of color, African American, Hispanic, Asian, but none had stuck. She had toyed with the idea of exploring intimacy with another woman in search of safety and security but had never had the patience nor felt the deep desire to do so. Heni was saddled with the expectation that she might never find a satisfactory alternative to lonely self-sufficiency and powered forward with her career.

Henry Hoary, of a similar age, was a native Ozarkian, born, bred, and educated within a fifty-mile geographical radius, and proud of it. He served as a student recruiter for a large regional university. He seemed secure in his job for the moment, although the business of recruiting and educating students of any age had ground to a near halt as communities large and small tried to get their arms around a deadly virus that no one seemed to have anticipated nor understood.

Henry had been married once, if being serially lied to and cheated on constituted marriage. It had lasted less than two years, the most miserable period of his life. So, he had taken to loving and leaving if things even drifted toward seriousness. He had broken hearts along the way, felt remorse on occasion, but never enough to risk a rerun.

Which is why beautiful Heni's advances had been so unexpected and unsettling. She just hadn't seemed the type.

Heni had met Henry in the checkout line of a small grocery store right after Heni had moved in on temporary assignment. Her boss had rented her a small town house for a month, wanting her to get a real feel for what was going on in the heartland and bring her own unique touch to sharing it. This was just days before the local "lockdown" had been ordered, essentially limiting access to anything beyond food, gas, drugs, and medical care. Heni had wondered if she should just hightail it back to the big city, but her boss encouraged her to stay and observe. Were citizens obeying "shelter in place" or slipping around at their own convenience? Was relief or anger the dominant response? Was local leadership communicating openly and honestly or ducking and weaving as each new case or death presented? Were local hospitals prepared for an influx of seriously sick patients or still stuck with trying to find masks and gowns? Were Springfield, Missouri, and Greene County ready or not? All this as best she could sense it on her limited forays out. As Heni and Henry social distanced with their masks, gloves, and selected items through the same checkout clerk, their eyes met and remet, almost smiling at each other. They carted to their respective vehicles, which happened to be facing; unloaded; turned out of the parking lot the same direction and into the same townhome development a short time later before parking literally next to each other. They were neighbors. At least for a while.

Henry finally worked up the nerve to ask Heni over for dinner. He had slipped a note of invitation underneath her front door, observing that going next door to dine surely fell into the list of permitted activities, if they distanced properly. He signed it Henry.

The return note observed that it likely did not, particularly with a total stranger, and was signed Heni. She added a PS wondering what could she bring. Heni was lonely and anxious to talk to a local about the many questions she was seeking answers for. And she had noticed in the few times their paths had crossed since shopping that his eyes were warm and penetrating above the cloth mask he generally wore.

Dinner was a welcome retreat from social isolation. Neither wore masks nor gloves, allowing a warmer interaction. They did stay strictly spaced apart.

Henry had barbecued chicken thighs on his small backyard grill along with thick slices of eggplant covered with shredded Parmesan cheese. He served a bottle of what appeared to be an expensive Tuscan blend to brighten the meal and evening. They drank and ate it all, laughing on occasion at the crazy things people seemed to be saying and doing these days and raising a toast to those on the front lines. They relaxed and enjoyed each other's company.

Heni invited Henry to join her the following evening. He obviously had nothing better to do and would have made up excuses if he had. He was enthralled with her extraordinary beauty, flashing eyes, and ready smile. Heni had made little progress in pursuing her list of questions, so a follow-up was only logical.

Dinner two was followed by a long walk the next morning, a beautiful specimen of spring in the Mozarks. They social distanced appropriately, horizontally when traffic allowed and one behind the other when not. Heni ceded the lead to Henry in those instances as he knew where they were going, and she frankly enjoyed watching his lean athletic figure move effortlessly from behind. Henry is a good-looking guy, she thought guardedly, not wanting to go beyond that casual observation.

Heni and Henry still made separate trips to the grocery store, generally at the same time, and soon began spending most evenings eating and drinking together and—at least once a day—walking, weather permitting. Social distancing shrunk.

As Heni and Henry got to know one another more personally, they each began to open up in their own way.

Henry reminisced about growing up next to his grandparents as a young lad in a small neighboring town. Life had been really good for him back then. His parents were loving and supporting and desirous of him receiving the best education he could, regardless of the financial sacrifices involved.

Heni shared the pain of her mother's poverty and sacrifice to provide her with those same basics, how it had made all the difference in allowing her to escape the cycle.

Henry shared the disaster this first marriage had been. Heni laughed at the notion of Henry's wife cheating on him with the minister who had married them and then felt badly about it. Henry shrugged a lighthearted forgiveness.

Their conversations got deeper and more personal as the days passed. Henry confessed to himself that he had allowed himself to fall in love for the first time since his divorce. Heni felt emotional most of the time when Henry was around. She wasn't sure this was a good thing.

That's why she surprised even herself when she had come on so brazenly to Henry in his backyard. It just wasn't like her. Reckless spontaneity had never been her thing. Something different was going on here.

"You know, I have never done anything like that before," Heni whispered in the wake of a rousing follow-up in Henry's bed.

"So, why me, beautiful Heni, why me?"

"I don't know, Henry. The times are strange, and most of us are disoriented in some way or another. But that is hardly an excuse for the wanton and impulsive behavior I exhibited."

"I think I am in love with you, Heni. I know I feel differently about you than anyone I have ever met, even though that was only a couple of weeks ago."

"How can you know something so important and personal as that in such a short time, Henry? I'm flattered, but I'm a single Black woman who you stumbled into at the local market, wined and dined with the finest night after night, and who simply seduced you in broad daylight to the applause of your neighbors. Where's the love in that, Henry?"

"Isn't that exactly what love is, Heni? An emotional urgency to be part of another and the willingness to take risks in pursuit of an unknown end?"

"So, what is the underlying story here, Henry? Let's forget about ourselves for the moment and trying to rationalize what we are all going through. I have a job to do. What can I share with my readers that no one else is covering? I am so sick of the same old reporting on casting blame, finger-pointing, inane political posturing, and manipulating the fears and emotions of a citizenry who are genuinely terrified or at least confused. What is more important? The health and well-being of seniors, the poor, and the physically compromised or jobs and the stock market? Is it really an either-or conundrum, or is that the whole point of the disruptors, to make it so? I've got to make my take different and important."

"Love is what's different, Heni. Love is the underlying story that will outlast any pandemic. Seek out and write about the love you find in this terrible moment in history. In our little town, our little region, our little part of the crazy world. Even in your own heart. You can change the names to protect the guilty. And since you have breached all social distancing and lockdown guidelines, unless sexual intercourse is considered an essential activity, I suggest we forego all future violations, and you move in with me for the remainder of your stay in the Mozarks. And maybe beyond?"

chapter three

THE NEWS

HENI AND HENRY INDEED AWOKE TOGETHER SEVERAL MORNINGS LATER, INTERTWINED in optimistic anticipation. No coughs, fevers, or shortness of breath in their bed.

Heni reluctantly pulled up her computer screen to see what was going on in a world she had briefly left behind and was supposed to be writing about. She gasped at what she saw.

"Henry, come fast. You won't believe this," Heni muttered as she began to scroll through a long front-page feature article from the *New York Times*.

PRESIDENT REVEALED
President of the United States' Secret Strategy for
Dealing with the Coronavirus Pandemic

It took a whistleblower from the president of the United States' small and subservient inner circle to collapse his house of faux cards around a global health pandemic. It also took great courage on the leaker's part, as this president is known for his vindictive nature and paranoid insistence on blind loyalty amongst his shills. His or her identify remains anonymous.

It first might be worthwhile to recall the president's incoherent babbling of the past couple of months about the virus, which would be almost laughable if so many lives were not at risk. His direct quotes as recorded in a recent *Times* piece:

1/22/20—" . . . we have it totally under control."
1/24/20—"It will all work out well."
1/30/20—"We have it very well under control."
2/2/20—"We've pretty much shut it down. . . ."
2/10/20—"In April, supposedly it dies."

2/14/20—"When it gets warm, it historically kills the virus."

2/25/20—" . . . getting better."

2/26/20—" . . . close to zero."

2/27/20—"One day—it's like a miracle—it will disappear."

2/28/20—" . . . then you'll be fine."

2/29/20—" . . . vaccine available very quickly. . . ."

3/3/20—" . . . cure."

3/4/20—"It's very mild . . . very small numbers."

3/6/20—"There is no testing kit shortage. . . . Anybody that wants a test can get a test. . . . I really like this stuff. I really get it."

3/7/20—"I'm not concerned at all."

3/10/20—"It will go away. Just stay calm. It will go away."

3/11/20—" . . . responding with great speed and professionalism."

3/12/20—" . . . going to go away."

3/13/20—"No, I don't take responsibility . . . all will be great."

3/17/20—"This is a pandemic. I felt it was a pandemic long before it was called a pandemic."

He really said these things. All in public, all recorded word for word. We now know why.

A hidden recording device switched to "on" in a major early strategy meeting between the president and several top advisers, while the virus was still confirmed in apparently manageable numbers in the continental US, lays out the tragedy for so many that was to come.

The New York Times has obtained the unedited transcript from a confidential source and presents it word for word below. It describes in great detail the president and key cabinet members' sinister strategy and tells all for the whole world to hear.

President: "Let me get this straight. If we do nothing as a country, just let this coronavirus wash over, we can get rid of a bunch of old farts who are depleting our social security trust fund; lots of colored citizens who never vote for us, anyway; the most destitute drags of many butthole countries around the world; and everyone else will eventually be OK? There will be no long-term economic crisis, the stock market will bounce back quickly, and my reelection will be assured? Is this succinct analysis correct?"

Cabinet Secretary A: "Yes, Mr. President, you are correct. The coronavirus disproportionately impacts the elderly and those living in poverty, especially Blacks and Hispanics. The death rates amongst those two population segments have already proven to be significantly higher across the globe. And once the young, productive, and healthy pass through it, we think they will be immune forever and can go straight back to work, jump-starting the economy, and returning the stock market to record levels."

President: "Does anyone know how the damn thing got started, anyway?"

Cabinet Secretary A: "Not for certain, Mr. President, but several Chinese scientists have leaked the theory that it originated from a rogue rectal infection in a herd of swine in Hunglow, China. That they may have eaten some 'bad mushrooms.'"

President: "I got into a batch of those my junior year in college. Really f'ed me up. Couldn't get an erection for almost a year. You can imagine what that did to my study habits. In fact I can't imagine any fate worse than living in a constant state of deflation.

"Speaking of which, what are we going to do about the stock market in the short term? It has plummeted even though the virus hasn't done much here. Why is that? The economy is stronger than ever, unemployment the lowest in half a century, and inflation nonexistent. Why the big sell off?"

Cabinet Secretary B: "Well, Mr. President, it has to do with everything from supply chain disruptions in sourcing countries that are starting to shut things down to canceled travel and vacation plans to the delayed impact of the tariffs you have imposed on our trading partners. There's just a lot of uncertainty all around Mr. President, here and abroad. And you know how markets hate uncertainty."

President: "OK, what can we do to fix it, Mr. Secretary?"

Cabinet Secretary A: "We can start by announcing strategies and policies to address what appears to be a growing international pandemic and global panic, Mr. President. We can take steps to stop its spread, and as they call it, flatten the mortality curve."

President: "Why would we do that? Why prolong the misery? This is the easiest decision I've had to make in four years. *We do nothing*. We let the coronavirus run its course, and we will all be better off in the long run. Kill off the elderly, the infirm, and the poor, here and around the world. Fewer parasites sucking on the welfare teat, less mouths to feed with foreign aid, more money to invest in dividends and the market."

Cabinet Secretary A: "Yes, sir, Mr. President. But with all due respect, we have to make it at least look like we are doing something or you will get lambasted in the short term."

President: "So, what might that be?"

Vice President: "Well, for starters, we could sit around and whistle "Dixie"? Might get you some extra votes in Alabama come November?"

President: I was thinking in terms of something a bit more creative, Mr. Vice President."

Cabinet Secretary A: "How about we—"

President: "I don't know what you are about to suggest Mr. Secretary, but be aware that I will approve nothing that could further damage the stock market. In fact we need to focus our actions on helping it recover. Quickly. And we need to take care of the business interests who support us. Got to keep them afloat so they can pay all the little people, and fund our reelection campaign."

Cabinet Secretary A: "I would recommend the following. First, we need to go to national lockdown. Keep everyone at home for a couple of weeks. That seems to be the gestation period for the virus to spread. Perhaps we can even determine if it is as lethal as the experts predict. Who knows? If other countries that are hurting now had done that sooner, they might be through the worst of it. And the doctors and scientists will like it."

President: "That's not going to keep businesses open and consumers spending stupid."

Cabinet Secretary A: "It's only in the short term, Mr. President, just to buy some time. Let's see if a lot of people die. If not, straight back to work. If so, burn the bodies and send the healthy ones back. They won't get it bad, if at all."

President: "Nope, we're not shutting down anything while I'm president."

Cabinet Secretary B: "OK, Mr. President. But we at least need to make our national stockpile of emergency medical supplies—things like masks, gowns, even ventilators—immediately available to hospitals in "red" communities and states, the people who elected you and will do so again because of your decisive actions to protect them. We need to be proactive in getting the goods to them."

President: "Well, that certainly leaves California and New York out of the equation. I kind of like that. So, how do we explain the shortfalls to them?"

Cabinet Secretary B: "Simple supply and demand, Mr. President. If we don't have goods in stockpile because of others' demand, we can't supply them. And if they want to buy them from states who have not squandered their resources, go for it. No votes lost there, anyway, in November."

President: "I like it, I really like it."

Cabinet Secretary C: "We also need to flood the national economy with liquidity. Free money to pay labor not to work and stay at home. So, they will have something to spend when we send them back out into the workplace."

President: "Can we afford it?"

Cabinet Secretary C: "Only in the short term, Mr. President. All of our actions are short term in nature to allow a return to long-term stability as soon as possible"

Cabinet Secretary A: Finally you need to tell everyone things will be all right. You need to provide reassurance that we have this virus under control, that a vaccine is just around the corner, that we may not even need that if the virus withers and dies with the coming of warmer weather. And just blame the Chinese, for God's sake. It's all their fault, and people generally need someone to direct their anger and frustration toward."

President: "Is any of this true?"

Cabinet Secretary A: Not that I am aware of, but you need to say anything to make folks feel better."

President: "What will the science geeks say?"

Cabinet Secretary A: "They won't like it, but it's not their job to publicly disagree. They will be politely respectful, and if they aren't, we'll just fire their asses. We have just got to reassure the country that things will be back to normal soon."

President: "Shouldn't be difficult."

Cabinet Secretary A: "Don't think so."

President: "This all sounds good to me. Again, only in the short term. What do you think, Mr. Vice President?"

Vice President: "I like short in everything from briefing papers to attention spans."

President: "I know, I know. And I'll put you in charge of everything, Mr. Vice President, so when anyone gets pissed, it will be at you—not me. You'll take one for the boss, won't you?"

Vice President: "Yes, sir."

Cabinet Secretary A: "It's a simple one-two-three-step process, Mr. President, that promises decisive action without needing to deliver, rewards your political base, and pumps the economy and stock market back to life with lots of cash and healthy, happy workers as soon as possible."

President: "And the rest of the world will get well eventually, with fewer mouths to feed and scrubbed populations to buy more 'Made in America' goods and services."

Cabinet Secretary C: "Exactly, Mr. President. A brilliant plan to deal with an unexpected election year complication. You need to share it, at least the eye candy part, with the rest of the nation."

As previously reported, the president's live address on television the following night did little to calm national and international jitters. He assured the audience that 'this is not a financial crisis," in his own words. His advisers reportedly cringed as his teleprompter read exactly the opposite and either he ad-libbed or misread. His call for calm and confidence in his government, his vague short-term policy recommendations, his declaration of war, his exhortations for greatness in times of challenge were met with skepticism by most. That he had rarely told the truth for over three years, let alone a lifetime, did not inspire confidence that he was about to begin to do so with any regularity.

Heni looked at Henry with eyes ablaze. "Now that's some real news!"

Her editor was on the phone with her before the morning was over.

"How's this playing out in your part of the world? I need some copy. Be careful out there."

"Back soon, boss."

chapter four

GETTING TO KNOW YOU

"YOU KNOW, HENRY, YOU ARE THE FIRST WHITE GUY I'VE EVER BEEN WITH," HENI whispered one morning.

"Well, is it true, hon, you know, what they say?"

"Don't be silly, Henry," Heni grimaced. "That's a racist comment, but I'll forgive you for now. So, what about you? Ever slept with one of my kind before?"

"I have never had sex with anyone so beautiful, so mysterious, so alluring, so—"

"I'm talking about Black, Henry, a Black woman?"

"You're not Black, Heni. You are ebony, your skin shines in sunlight, and your eyes sparkle and dance when you are animated. I will never forget that first time, when you stood and stripped bare naked in the sinking sun and lit up the whole backyard—"

"Answer the question, Henry. Have you ever made love to a woman of color before, a Black woman?"

"Heni, I've decided I've never made love to anyone before you. It wasn't love. It was sex, it was pleasure, it was occasionally boring, but it was not making love. No, not until you."

"OK, I give up."

"The answer to your question is no."

"I've got to get some interviews with locals, Henry, about the president and his shit. Can you help me?"

"Well, you can you start with me? I promise not to tell all—"

"Enough, Henry, enough. Yes, I will start with you. How about right now? And cut the silly stuff. This is serious. Are you ready?"

"Ready."

"Thanks for agreeing to meet with me, sir. What is your name, please, and what do you normally do for a living?

"I'm sorry, young lady, but I prefer to remain anonymous and will speak to you on that basis only."

Heni looked puzzled but proceeded. "Why, if I may ask, sir?"

"I'm afraid. Not of you, not of the virus. You are sitting a proper six feet away from me as we speak, both with masks and gloves on. No, it is not you. I'm afraid of just about everything. Particularly after the big reveal regarding the president of the United States. I don't trust him or what he might do to protect his chair in the White House."

"Good, sir. May we talk about the president and your perceptions of his leadership in this time of crisis?"

"The president has never been a leader. The past three months of tragic pandemic mismanagement have only highlighted this. He's been a char-latan in business, on TV, as a presidential candidate, and from day one as president. He has no core, no credibility, no morality, no judgement, all critical attributes of an effective leader."

"You have mentioned fear more than once."

"It is the dominant emotion I feel every day."

chapter five

TRUTH AND CONSEQUENCES

AMIDST THE CHAOS OF THE *NEW YORK TIMES* BLOCKBUSTER RELEASE, THE PRESIDENT screamed fake news, fraud, and accused Democrats of plotting to overturn the will of the people. The Democrats, in turn, talked about impeachment for the second time in two years.

It was reported by an inside observer that he immediately fired every one of the key advisers who had been in the room with him for that initial coronavirus strategy meeting. The notes this observer shared with the press documented the process, including a bizarre exchange with the vice president:

"You can't fire me, Mr. President. The people elected me."

"No, they didn't, idiot. I selected you to be vice president. They elected me. You're fired. You get it? You are fired."

"But I didn't do anything wrong. I didn't record our meeting or leak it to the press."

"Well, one of you assholes did, and until I find out who, I don't trust any of you. I've asked the CIA to look into it. Can't trust the FBI. We need to ferret out the true traitor to me and to our nation and do it quickly. For now, you all are fired!"

"Oh."

Over the next several weeks, Henry and Heni looked on and listened in disbelief as the coronavirus continued to spread exponentially through the nation and the world, leaving death in its wake. Mostly old. Mostly impoverished.

"Henry, what is most frightening is that the president of the United States' grand scheme of 'doing nothing' in order to rid he world of its weakest could have slipped by, except for the bravery of one close adviser who blew the whistle loudly and clearly. Now, there is at least a chance to intervene and alter the trajectory of this tragedy. If it is not already too late. What can possibly happen next?"

"Well, some countries have gotten their stuff together and are actually slowing the rates of infection and death. And as with some other locales around the country, the extension of our own community's lockdown and required masking seem to have preempted a spike locally. Holding the course seems critical. On a broader front, the Democrats are moving to impeach the president, and the voters will have a chance in the fall to reject him. Neither have been successful to date."

"It seems like the divide screams even louder than the voices on either side."

"You need to write that one down, Heni. You have captured the whole essence of our problems in that simple statement. Send it to your editor immediately."

"What if he orders me home, Henry?"

"If you keep providing him with provocative interviews and juicy quotes like that, he will do well to leave you be."

"I'm not sure I could leave you, Henry. This is the happiest month I have spent in my life, despite what is going on outside it."

"I'm in love with you, Heni, and I will never let you go."

They rose in unison and embraced fiercely, clinging on for several minutes.

"You've got to line up some more locals for me to interview, Henry. At least one in-depth and daily. From all points of view. That is my ticket for 'sheltering in' with you for a while."

chapter six

PASSING TIME

TIME PASSED. ONE MONTH THEN TWO. SPRING SLID INTO SUMMER. THE COMMUNITY began to reopen, generally masked, and without serious incidence of infection. It never had reached high in the case count numbers or beyond double digits in deaths. Stay-at-home orders and masks had served their short-term purpose of preventing a massive breakout. Midsummer heat was expected to further mitigate that end, though no one could be sure until it came to pass.

Deniers were fierce in their criticism of the gradual opening up of things deemed nonessential and being forced to wear masks. Both were an infringement on their personal rights. "It is my right as a citizen of the United States to live as I wish."

"Right to die, right to infect, right to kill?" was the common rebuttal.

The biggest battle loomed over places of worship. Springfield is a churchgoing community. Big churches. Megachurches. Some of Heni's most provocative interviews were with parishioners who were desperate to return to their pews. God would protect if they had faith and paid proper homage. Her editor loved it and begged for more.

Many other interviewees spoke to fear, like Henry did. Some feared that things would never be the same again. Others feared that they would go right back where they had been when it was all over. It generally spoke to one's station in life. Heni guessed both were valid with their fears.

On the national front, the dying and spreading of cases continued in pockets of least resistance. The president railed on about conspiracies and fake news, but only his most stubborn admirers stayed tuned. Without his incoherent rants in large venues, which most cities kept closed, his visibility and commotion quotient languished.

As did the economy. Some people returned to their previous employment, though many small businesses that had shuttered remained so.

The opposition chose to drop divisive public hearings on treason and impeachment and focus time and resources on the coming election. It was essential that the country be rid of its neofascist leader and those who protected him out of fear of retribution. New and progressive leadership was needed, as was the turnover of a corrupt legislative branch. It would not be easy, particularly given the financial resources the president and his apologists had amassed.

Summer in the Mozarks is a time to head for water. Lakes, streams, creeks, pools. Finally one constant remains the same mid-corona.

"Have you ever been on a float trip, Heni?"

"A what?"

"Guess that answers my question. You load up a canoe with a cooler of beer, a fishing pole, and just float it down a clear, rippling creek on a sunlit day. Not a care in the world, no one else around, just you and me and the beauty of the Mozarks. And if you get too hot, just throw off your clothes and jump in to refresh."

"Sounds dangerous, Henry."

"Can be if the water is too high, fast, and brown or the weather forecast calls for a tornado."

"What if you turn over?"

"You take a swim in the cold, clear water, after you grab the cooler and the fishing pole, of course. Dump the canoe, and get back in."

"I don't know, Henry. I never learned how to swim. I don't want to drown in some far-out creek in Southwest Missouri. Corona is enough risk for me right now."

"Come on, give it a try. A life jacket will cover that. I'll take care of you, and you will love it."

chapter seven

ESCAPE

"OK, HENI. LET'S ESCAPE FROM THIS MESS OF A WORLD WE INHABIT. GO ON A FLOAT trip with me this weekend. We can even spend a night camping out. I've got all of the equipment, and the weather is supposed to be warm and beautiful."

"You mean we actually sleep on the ground?"

"No, a gravel bar, on top of a pad, all snuggled in a sleeping bag with me. After we make love under the stars."

"You have got to be kidding me."

It was a beautiful warm day, just as Henry had promised, when they loaded a canoe in the back of his pickup truck, along with tent, cooler, sleeping bags, grill, food, beer, wine, and coffee, and set off for Henry's favorite off-the-beaten-path stream an hour-and-a-half away. They drove in separate vehicles so as to leave one at the take-out spot before driving upstream to launch.

"This is everything you said it would be." Heni smiled over her shoulder an hour after put-in.

A leisurely pace, a few fighting smallmouth bass, a light shore lunch, and a couple of beers later, Heni actually fell asleep sitting slumped in the front of the canoe. Henry could only smile deeply.

He found a beautiful gravel bar next to a nice bathing hole late afternoon and pulled in to set up camp. They gathered firewood, erected the tent, unrolled sleeping gear into it, built a roaring fire to cook steaks on, and settled comfortably in lawn chairs, Heni with a paper cup of red wine, Henry with his normal Corona Light.

"Why do you insist on drinking Corona during the pandemic?"

"I don't know, just kind of thumbing my nose at it, I guess. Call it a protest."

"Seems kind of weird to me, but who am I to complain to the man who has given me one of the more memorable days of my life?"

"Well, it's about to get more memorable," Henry smiled, glancing at the tent.

Amidst the banter and early evening sounds around the crackling campfire, a staccato noise interrupted. It was definitely not natural. Soon a four-wheeler pulled up onto the gravel bar from behind. It was driven by a heavyset man in overalls and a straw hat. He stopped the motor and looked around at the campsite, then at Henry and Heni.

"What the hell do you all think you are doing?"

Henry shrugged and responded, "Enjoying a beautiful evening alongside a beautiful creek, sir." He sensed trouble.

"Well, you need to pack up and move along."

"Why?"

"First and foremost because I don't allow no niggers on my land, and your lady friend sure appears to be one."

"Pardon me, sir." Henry started rising slowly. "But this gravel bar belongs to the creek not you, as I understand it. And I will not allow you to insult my friend."

"Look, son, I will be back in one hour, just before it turns dark, with my shotgun and my two dogs. You had better have your white ass, your nigger whore, and all of the rest of this shit far downstream if you don't want serious trouble. This is my land, my rules, and my only warning."

He started the engine, backed off the gravel bar, and spun out into the woods along a dirt path.

Henry sat in stunned silence. "I am so sorry, Heni. In all my years of floating and camping along this creek, nothing remotely like this has ever happened."

"Well, you obviously never had a Black woman with you before, Henry."

Heni's countenance reflected anger and fear. "Let's get out of here, Henry, before someone gets hurt."

"It's not that easy, hon, we've got to find a place to settle in before dark and set all of this up again. But I agree."

Thirty minutes later, Henry shoved the loosely loaded canoe into the current and squinted into the darkening shadows downstream. He would have to find another gravel bar soon.

As night closed in, he guessed wrong going into a tricky rapid, strayed too close to a line of willow trees, caught the bow in a root wad, and rolled the canoe into the churning water. Heni screamed and hugged her life jacket. Henry started to grab the gear but quickly refocused on Heni, grabbing her from behind as she bounced into the dark hole of water below the rapid. She was sobbing and shaking as he pulled her near.

"It's OK, love, I have you now." He turned to see his canoe wrap around a rock midstream, as gear and cooler drifted beyond. He finally found creek bottom and walked up into the wooded bank.

"I need to get something for us to sleep in, something to warm us up," he muttered to Heni, leaning back toward the water.

"Don't leave me, Henry, do not leave me here by myself. You promised to take care of me, and you've done a pretty piss-poor job so far."

Henry looked longingly downstream, then back at his wounded canoe, and returned to take shivering Heni in his arms. "I sorry. I am so sorry."

They stayed that way for the rest of the longest, coldest night of their lives.

chapter eight

RECOVERY

"**H**ENRY, DO YOU THINK THAT OLD RELIC OF RACISM REALLY WOULD HAVE KILLED US?"
"I don't know, Heni, I am just so sorry. For you to be subjected to such hatred and vitriol, threatened with your life, and suffer through near-drowning and discomfort of epic proportions because of me is unforgivable. I don't know. I have never felt lower than this in my life. And you, I can't imagine what you are feeling? About me? About the Mozarks? About the creek I love so much?"

Heni and Henry were lying together in bed, late afternoon. Still occasionally shivering with cold and fear. Not quite touching but closer than earlier.

Heni finally snuggled in. "Don't be so tough on yourself, Henry. You didn't put my life at risk. Fate did. You saved it. You didn't let me get shot. You didn't let me drown. You didn't let me freeze to death. You walked me out of the woods early this morning to the car and delivered me safely home to a hot shower. It wasn't a pleasant experience but one we survived."

"You know we have to go back and fetch my truck at the place we put in, don't you?

"Can I wear a paper sack over my head in case we see ol' Redneck Rectum again?"

This set them both to laughing.

As they lay in the quiet, Heni asked again, "Do you think he really would have killed us?

"I don't know. There is just so much hatred all around."

"I know, Henry, I know."

"It took less than one term for an isolationist, racist, misogynist, nativist president vowing to 'Make America Great Again' to feed a xenophobic fury amongst his base supporters that has divided America more than at any time since the long-ago and inappropriately named Civil War. A state of mind in which our redneck yahoo still seems to dwell. How it could have happened so fast is beyond understanding, though one can only conclude that the Grand Facilitator and his poster children represent a long simmering undercurrent of hatred and despair amongst a small but intense non-racial or non-gendered minority that has finally hissed out, like a dormant volcano gone live. Sorry for the diatribe. Yes, he might have killed us."

Post "Do-Nothing Gate" analysis.

Even the President's staunchest supporters and defenders tried to distance themselves from the greatest presidential train wreck in history, and the angry mood of a nation sick and deceived pushed them there.

The subsequent election results appeared to rid the country of its national nightmare, though the suffering he had imposed in such a short time would linger a long time. With *appeared* the operative word.

Three days following his election loss, the president declared a national emergency based on a Russian dissident cell's confession of guilt to cyber intrusion in ballot counting in multiple key states to ultimately throw the election to his opponent. The confession was obtained by, released, and corroborated by the Kremlin, which pledged to more rigorously combat interference in foreign sovereign elections in the future and to work closely with the president to combat the international health crisis. The timing, the content, the irony of a newly minted love affair with Russia were so absurd as to be laughable to most.

Nonetheless, with his declaration of a national emergency, the president claimed wartime powers and refused to concede defeat, backed voraciously by his base. A new and fair election would be scheduled as soon as the coronavirus was under control. Until then, it would be business as usual, and he would calmly lead his country through the crisis and back to unparalleled economic security. And subsequently reelection.

Amidst the chaos that followed, both houses of Congress called on the secretary of defense to depose the president, who remained ensconced in the White House, claiming a voluntary quarantine to protect himself from the virus at this time of national emergency.

The secretary of defense refused to intervene on direct orders from his commander-in-chief, as the clock ticked down on 2020.

Heni's editor was now on the phone with her daily, if not more, begging for a heartland read on the cascade of unparalleled events playing out before a physically and emotionally sickened world's eyes. She was glad that he had stopped asking if she minded staying another week or two. Heni and Henry were having the love-in of their lives.

The president himself holed up in the White House with members of his immediate family for nearly three months, continuously threatening to launch a nuclear attack on China in retaliation for their birthing of the plague if anyone tried to depose him. Theoretically, the secretary of defense was required to "cosign" any such strike, but given his apparent aversion to confronting the presidential takeover, few felt he could be trusted to circumvent presidential orders.

The president surrounded the grounds with his most rabid white supremacist supporters, armed to the teeth, with orders to fire on anyone who approached the fenced perimeter, excepting of course those from his base who were preparing and delivering food and drink. Both houses of Congress, the Supreme Court, and his duly elected successor declared his actions illegal, but no one dared risk a nuclear conflagration, which all agreed he was unhinged enough to deliver.

The FBI was finally able to infiltrate his food source battalion and slip psychedelic mushrooms into a pasta sauce, which rendered the president and his family incapacitated enough by hallucinations for agents to reclaim the "nuclear football" briefcase from his possession, dispose of his "biscuit" or authorizing code, and apprehend him.

Tweeting "coupe, coupe, coupe," as his senses cleared and he was put under lock and key, the disgraced former president of the United States was hustled out of the public eye.

And a new president of the United States stepped up with promises to conquer the coronavirus and put communities back to work again. America would reunite and reengage with the world and reality in that quest and the slow recovery that would surely follow. She had specific short- and long-term strategies to implement with the support of both houses of Congress and other leaders around the globe. She promised that the United States would again provide vision, leadership, collaboration, and money to rebuild trust and trade.

All of this stranger-than-fiction-playing-out-as-real-life provided Heni with interview topics she could never have conceived of in her journalistic career. From the coronavirus popping up with a vengeance to an unhinged president of the United States, who incidentally fared unconscionably well with some interviewees, Heni flooded her editor with perspectives that sold copy.

And still no vaccine. Not enough tests. No reliable verification of antibodies curing or preventing the disease. Ten, twelve months in, the international scientific community simply didn't know enough yet to definitively stop it. Until Henrietta White ultimately broke a story for the ages.

When Heni and Henry sat around at night with wine and Corona Light, neither could really comprehend what had brought them together so quickly and solidly in love and respect. They began their second spring together above and beyond the continuing corona crisis.

chapter nine

LIFE

"I THINK I'M PREGNANT, HENRY. I'VE MISSED TWO PERIODS AND FEEL UNFAMILIAR stirrings inside. I have been afraid to tell you and to get a test, but guess it's finally time for both."

Henry's smile lit up the room. "I'm so excited, Heni. Will you marry me? I'll get down on one knee and promise never to take you on a float trip again. Will you be my wife and never leave me?"

"Does the offer still stand if there is no little one on the way?"

"Yes. Now and forever."

The pregnancy test read positive. A real live coronalove baby was on the way.

Hobart cradled Ethel's head in his lap. Her fever burned through his overalls. She moaned lightly and began coughing again. It was a brittle cough, as if bugs were trying to crawl out of her sunken chest.

"I've got to take you in, Ethel. Doc Evans told me that a week ago if you didn't get better. You've gotten worse. You're not gonna make—"

Hobart sobbed deeply, tears flushing his cheeks. "Ethel, please listen to me. You are burning up and are going to die of this coronavirus unless I get you to a hospital emergency room right now."

Ethel leaned up and into Hobart's chest. She looked deeply into his eyes and weakly spat out, "No, Hobe. I ain't going nowhere to die alone."

"But, Ethel—"

"Take me to the creek, Hobart. I'm burning up and want you to lay me in it to cool me down."

Hobart nodded slowly and lifted her tiny frail frame into his arms. He walked out the back door and down a short hill to Crane Creek and waded into the headwaters spring that fed it. He sat in the frigid water and laid Ethel back down on his lap. She shivered, closed her eyes, then sighed deeply.

The welts were discernible on Henry's left flank. His scratching had left them raised and red.

"Does that feel as ugly as it looks?" asked Heni.

"You are no longer drawn to my finely chiseled body, Ms. Heni? You didn't seem to mind it so much last night before dinner?"

"I love your body, Henry, you know that. It's those bites or whatever on your butt that I was noticing."

"Yep, I'm itching like crazy. Started a couple of nights ago, actually waking up mornings is when I notice them. They itch, I scratch, they go away, and then some new ones show up. You think maybe I'm getting mosquito bites on our walks?"

"On your butt? Not likely," countered Heni.

After several more episodes Heni got online. She wasn't sure what she was looking for but ran the gamut from mosquitos to ticks to fleas to dust mites to . . . bedbugs. Bingo.

"Check out these bites, Henry. Anything look familiar."

"What are they?"

"Bedbug bites."

A quick call to the condo manager was referred to his pest specialist, who was too busy to stop by for several days but advised them to look in their sheets and particularly along the edges of their mattress for any type of dead bugs. They did so and found several clusters of dark matter on the mattress. When they reported in, he asked them to email a cell phone photo immediately. His return call launched an improbable nightmare of inconvenience and expense more intrusive, at least in their case, than any virus could present.

"You definitely have bedbugs and need to take action right now. Go to the store and get rolls of plastic wrap, enclose your mattress, bed frame, and every piece of bedding. Place it all out on the front curb, and I will have someone pick up and destroy. Wash and dry all clothing in your bedroom on high heat and place in trash bags. Same with shoes and miscellaneous items. "

"You've got to be kidding" whined Henry in disbelief.

"I'm dead serious, sir. We can only hope they haven't transited to your living room, where you will live until I can get there to apply treatment."

"Can we go to a hotel?"

"No, you could be putting them at risk, and besides most are shuttered during the lockdown."

"Can we stay with a friend?"

"Again, you would be potentially spreading this to them. Doubt you want to do that, do you?"

"So, when can you get here to spray them?"

"I'm sorry but not until the middle of next week. Too much going on with this pandemic and all. Let's say Wednesday. And you will need to be out of the condo for at least six hours, depending on how hard I have to blast it."

"Can we even slip in to use the toilet?"

"Nope. Sorry again."

"Where do we go?"

"How about the great outdoors? And I almost forgot. You will have to stay out of your bedroom for a week following my treatment."

"You mean we get to camp out in our living room for almost two weeks and sleep on the floor?"

"Yes."

"One more question, if you will. My fiancée lives with me and, to our knowledge, has not been bitten once. How can that be?"

"The critters simply like some folks and not others."

When Henry relayed the bad news to Heni, she could only shrug her shoulders in disbelief and pat her small baby bump for comfort.

"Guess we're going to get to know each other even better over the next two weeks."

"Not all bad," replied Henry.

"Incidentally, how did he answer that last question, the one about me not getting any bites?"

"Well, it seems that the little buggers like some folks better than others."

A wry grin crept across Heni's face.

"Even the bugs down her in the Mozarks are racists."

This set them both to laughing. They were going to have to draw deeply on humor to smooth the edges of this next aberration in their shared lives.

chapter ten

HOBART AND ETHEL

HOBART AND ETHEL CAMPBELL HAVE BEEN MARRIED FOR MORE THAN FIFTY YEARS. They first met in high school in Lodi, California. Their parents were transplants from the Midwest and engaged in farming. Lodi was a small community in California's Central Valley located on a railroad line. Its moderate weather, transportation availability, and proximity to San Francisco contributed to a laid-back but affordable lifestyle. It became a major wine producing center over the years, but Hobert and Ethel were long gone by then.

They eloped upon graduating from school, deeply and totally engaged in one another, and anxious to escape the small-town simplicity of their upbringing. Southern California called, and they spent their first twenty years of life together moving around Los Angeles. Hobart got involved in the aircraft production industry as a line worker and then supervisor. He made good money. Ethel became an elementary school teacher and didn't. Still, together they managed to save enough to buy a house in the San Fernando Valley and live comfortably, as their residence appreciated in value exponentially. Ethel tried to become a mother, but it just wasn't going to happen. It would be just she and Hobart to the end of their days, and that fact of life drew them even closer together.

As L.A. grew and congested, they began to tire of the crowds and congestion. Over a glass of wine one evening, coincidentally from a Lodi sourced bottle, Hobart threw out a revolutionary idea.

"Let's reverse migrate, Ethel."

"What in the world are you talking about, Hobe?"

"Let's move back to small-town Missouri, where our folks came from, and become farmers like they were."

"You're kidding," Ethel responded in disbelief.

"Think about it, Ethel. All we have in this life is each other. No children. No parents that give much of a hoot about us. Just you and me."

"Come on, my mom left us a nice inheritance nest egg."

"That's true, and it has provided us with some financial security. Still, this life we are living is so bland. We each get up every morning, drive through the maddening mess of traffic, to the same boring places, back home eight hours later, still get frisky on occasion—but I sometimes wonder if that is more boredom than affection —and just repeat the loop again. If we don't do something different, we'll just be sitting here twenty years from now wondering why we didn't."

"I can't believe you are saying this, Hobart Campbell. First of all, you might find me boring, but you still turn me on."

"I didn't mean it that way, hon. It was just all part of a metaphor."

"That's a big word, Hobe. Did you learn that at Lodi High School while you were sneaking around trying to take my bra off? You didn't find that so damn boring, particularly when I let you do it."

"Come on, Ethel, I'm just trying to paint a picture of a lifestyle that seems stuck in so many ways. It's not you. I love you more than anything ever. But I don't love the rut we are stuck in. I want to be free of crowds and the routine. I want to grow something, to bring something to life, to contribute to others, not a corporate giant's bottom line."

"You really are serious, aren't you?"

"Yep. Are you in?"

"Oh, Hobe. I think you are crazy. But I will go anywhere, do anything, with you. You know that. I don't know about farming, but I bet we can find a place that needs a good pre-K or elementary school teacher. When do we jump off the cliff?"

"My dad's brother, Uncle Elmer, lives in Missouri, the southwest part I believe, something called the Ozarks. Let me check in with him for ideas about how to proceed."

"Are you really talking Ozarks, as in hillbillies? Like the Beverly Hillbillies? Overalls, corncob pipe, and all?"

"Yeah, can't you just see me and Jethro sipping whiskey out of a jug together?"

Several months and half a dozen phone calls later, Hobart Campbell submitted his retirement papers and put their house on the market. Their timing could not have been better. Elmer Campbell, who had lost his wife several years earlier, had fallen into ill health. He was trying to sell his farm, which sat near a big headwaters spring of some creek named Crane, and move into a retirement complex in Springfield. His property had been on the market for several months but was deemed priced too high by most locals. Not by L.A. standards.

Ethel and Hobart took a long weekend and flew back to take a look. The house was simple, but the spring and small creek it looked over from a knoll above was pristine and gorgeous. Taken together, the property checked every box on Hobart and Ethel's wish list. It was remote yet close to a small town and within an hour of a significant metropolitan area in Southwest Missouri.

There was no haggling over price. Seller got what he wanted. Buyers likewise. Timing was the only issue as Hobart and Ethel would need to sell their San Fernando Valley property before they could close on the deal. Elmer proposed renting his house to them for a nominal amount until that could happen. He had no need for cash, no debt on his farm, which really wasn't a functioning farm. A few chickens and a henhouse for eggs dotted the side yard. He assured Hobart that he could earn a living fixing things for people around the county, something Hobart was good at after all of his years in the production line. And Ethel could indeed get a teaching job. With their nest egg and the equity in their L.A. home, life would be good on their Crane Creek paradise.

Thirty years later, they were living the dream and had become happy hillbillies. Until she got the virus, shopping at Walmart in Springfield.

Ethel stirred slightly in Hobart's shivering arms. He had held her like this, suspended in the water, for over an hour, and was beginning to worry about hypothermia. For him, not her.

He had watched in amazement as she settled into the cool waters, fever flush receding, cough halting, peace filling her face. He couldn't dare move without risk of regression. At least that is what he reasoned until he simply couldn't stand the cold any more. His extremities were numb, and his whole body ached. Hobart had to do something.

He finally rose, tried to loosen his stiff legs enough to walk, and pulled Ethel close to his trembling body. He moved slowly out of the water and toward the warmth of their back door in the cool spring air. Up the hill he trudged, one step at a time, hoping against hope that he was strong enough to make it without falling. He was.

Once inside, he crawled next to the fire he had left blazing, threw a couple more logs on it, and pulled an old blanket off the couch to wrap them up in.

Ethel opened her eyes and smiled. "It's a miracle, Hobe. I'm not hot anymore, and I can breathe without coughing. The creek has saved me."

Hobart could only shake his head and draw her closer. He had never really believed in miracles, even of the biblical brand, but what he had just witnessed was undeniable. He could never tell anyone or they would commit him to the loony bin and he would never see Ethel again.

chapter eleven

ED

ED JONES WAS A BAD MAN. A REALLY BAD MAN. HE WAS THE KIND OF BAD MAN WHO would take a hammer to one headlight of a parked automobile, throw his dog's feces into a neighbor's backyard, and occasionally deposit roadkill on a random front porch. All sneaky stuff, generally under the cover of darkness, intended to irritate and play with the mind of a normal human being.

Ed justified his evil ways by quoting the Bible. Ed was bad but not dumb. He had read the Good Book from cover to cover no less than ten times over the past several years and could cite chapter and verse in defense of his actions. That is what Ed really liked about the Bible. There was something there for any one or any act, no matter how vile.

Ed's favorite was "an eye for an eye." (Exodus 21:24). In Ed's eyes this granted him holy authority to do anything he damn well pleased to any-one because everyone had always had it out for him and had for his entire life. He was simply trading his hurt eye for one of theirs that he could hurt.

He also loved the story of King David sending his top general, Uriah, to the front lines of war . . . so he could be killed in battle and the good king could take Bathsheba, Uriah's beautiful wife whom he had impregnated, for his own. (2 Samuel 11:2–5, 15–17) This clearly justified Ed taking any woman he wanted, by any means, no matter how devious.

Another favorite was the "bottomless pit" (Revelation 9:1-2), where he hoped all who ridiculed or ignored him would end up. And Cain killing his brother Abel and asking if he was his brother's keeper (Genesis 4:8–9). "Hell, no," Ed loved to scream into the mirror late at night. His inventory of biblical rationalizations for his aberrant behavior was endless.

Ed had no conscience nor concern for anyone but himself. He lived out this philosophy in alternating cycles of violence then abstinence.

Unfortunately, Ed lived in the same townhome subdivision that Henry and Heni were holed up in, just six doors removed. He also shopped at the same small grocery store that they did and pumped gas from the same filling station they frequented. And, worse yet, he had a terrible crush on Heni. He had silently observed that first love-in scene in Henry's backyard with envy and jealously. He had marveled at her beauty and grace and wanted her desperately.

Despite his sick personality, Ed presented well physically and verbally.

When these urges had happened with other women over the years, he had generally gotten his way. On those occasions when he had been successful in seducing a victim, he had generally tired of them quickly and moved on. He had only needed to hurt a couple of them.

He decided that if he was to have a chance with this beautiful Black lady, whose full name (Henrietta) he had learned from raiding Henry's mailbox and finding an occasional piece addressed to her, he would have to make their life together very uncomfortable. He spied on them quietly yet intrusively, learning many secrets that they shared, intent on disrupting their best laid plans. He envied their passionate physical relationship, and while Henrietta's pregnancy threw a wrinkle in Ed's desire to have her for his own, it only added a timeliness to his efforts. He sure didn't desire some eight-month-along pregnant mother to be his next conquest, but if he could break them up soon, there would be plenty of time to enjoy her dark, taut, supple body before it bloated with baby.

Ed started by messing with Henrietta's car in subtle ways. He was well trained in breaking into a car and even had the official law enforcement aids to pop locks. Lights would be turned on to drain the battery. Hoses would be pricked to allow leakage of fluids from beneath the hood. Strange puncture wounds to tires would allow air to release slowly and eventually flatten. All of this did add inconvenience to their lives but not enough to get them fussing.

It was when he found a scourge in his own unit that he cheerfully decided to share it to their great discomfort. Bedbugs. Ed didn't know how he had gotten the infestation, probably the hooker he had hired in the week before, but their presence became physically obvious. He had suffered through a bedbug siege before and knew exactly what he was looking at. What a housewarming gift they would make. So, instead of burning his sheets, he carefully folded one of them up, placed it on Henry's front doormat, and rang the doorbell.

Henry casually picked up the neatly folded bundle and carried it into his bedroom, assuming that Heni had left it there for him to take inside while she was out shopping and wondering who had rung. When she returned several hours later, she saw the folded sheet lying on their bed and shook it out, thinking Henry had intended to put it on their bed for some reason or another.

The rest is history.

chapter twelve

THE CREEK

"TELL ME ABOUT THIS CRANE CREEK, HENRY. MY EDITOR ASKED ME TO LOOK INTO IT for a possible story. He read about it and some of the unique creatures it plays host to in some regional environmental magazine, *Mollyjagger*, or something like that. Strange things like giant water moccasins, four to five feet long, and some rare species of trout. I never thought I would ever want to go back to a creek, no matter how beautiful and unique, again after our run-in with that old redneck."

Henry laughed and confirmed that he had spent a fair amount of time on Crane Creek in his youth, fishing for those fabled trout and trying to avoid the snakes.

"So, what is a water moccasin, Henry?"

"You mean they didn't have any of those in your St. Louis ghetto?" Henry saw Heni cringe and quickly apologized. "I am so sorry, Heni,
I didn't mean to offend."

"It wasn't so much offending as remembering. Language and words slip into conversations with racial undertones that carry multiple meanings. No harm intended, I know. If I didn't know you as I do, I might have been pissed. And, no, we didn't have any five- or six-foot snakes in the 'hood growing up. Well, actually we did, and if Crane Creek snakes are as mean as some of characters of my youth, I want to stay well away from them."

"You won't encounter a meaner critter than a water moccasin, Heni. I've never been bitten by one, but they can paralyze a man or even kill him. One old fishing guide I used to hang out with swore that he even had one stalk him one night, trying to hunt him down like a frog or a lizard. They are also called cottonmouths because, when they rare up to strike, it looks like their gullets are full of cotton."

"Ugh."

"Look, Heni, we've got to be out of our place for most of the day tomorrow while they blast away at the little bedbug bastards. Why don't I drive you down to Crane Creek for a look-see? There was a really nice old guy who owned a farm he used to let me access the creek through, with the most beautiful spring right down from his back door. I bet he would let us fish and look around a bit. Think I recall his last name was Campbell? Yes, Mr. Campbell. He might even let you interview him."

"I'm game, Henry."

Henry knocked on the door. A woman answered.

"Afternoon, ma'am. I am looking for Mr. Campbell. I was going to call but couldn't locate a phone number."

"Hobe, there is young man here looking for you."

"I remember you, son. You used to come out and fish our waters for McClouds, didn't you?

"Yes, Mr. Campbell, and you kindly let me have ready access. I'm Henry Hoary, and I've got my fiancée, Henrietta White, with me today. She's a journalist with a regional magazine and has been asked by her editor to do a piece on Crane Creek and its unusual cast of characters. She would love to have an opportunity to wander around the creek, see if I can show her a real McCloud trout, and maybe even interview you and the missus about your life on Crane Creek."

"Well, by all means on all accounts, Henry. Fishing's been a little slow this spring because of high waters I'm told. I don't get out much anymore, and there's really not much traffic down here. Nice to see someone. We've been stuck inside because the wife came down with the virus several weeks back. She is lucky to be alive."

"She survived the coronavirus, Mr. Campbell?"

"That's for sure. Thank God."

"And Crane Creek," added Ethel.

Hobart looked at his wife sternly, with a quiet "Shush."

"Have your lady friend come in, and we'll give you a cold drink before you set out."

Three hours later, Henry and Heni were back.

"No luck with the McClouds, Mr. Campbell. No cottonmouths, either. Just an amazing hike along a beautiful spring-fed creek in a pristine and rare landscape. Do you think my friend Heni could ask you a few questions about your life here in this paradise? She won't take long or be too intrusive."

"Sure. Shoot, Ms. White."

"Well, you can start with telling me more about these unusual trout."

"They are beautiful creatures, I'm so sorry you couldn't hook into one today. Very skittish as well. Never too large, but with a bright red slash of color down their side, which distinguishes them from other wild trout. And they are wild."

"What do you mean, Mr. Campbell? Wild?"

"Well, they breed on their own and have in Crane Creek for nearly 150 years. Other Missouri trout don't. They are a subspecies of rainbow trout. The Missouri Fisheries Commission stocked McCloud River trout in Crane Creek and several other sites around the state in the late 1800s. These still survive and thrive."

"Why? Is it because of Crane Creek?"

"Well, some attribute mysterious magical qualities to Crane Creek."

"I do," interrupted Ethel.

"Quite, hon," Hobart interrupted back, again with a disapproving shake of his head. Heni took note and glanced at Henry in puzzlement.

"Crane Creek is unique, in that it supports a large spectrum of life in a very short and narrow watershed. It is only twenty-three miles long, birthed and fed by cold, clear springs bubbling from limestone karst. At places along its course, it is barely ten feet wide."

"Slow down, Mr. Campbell. You are dealing with a city slicker here. What is limestone karst?"

"Sorry Ms. White—"

"Please call me Heni, Mr. Campbell."

"Sure, Heni. It is the nature of our subsurface rock in the Ozarks. Very porous, think of Swiss cheese. It allows rain and other water to percolate through it, cleansing as it goes, into the purest of water tables beneath, birthing crystal springs, which feed into the sparkling creek you just tromped through. Not very scientific and probably more than you ever wanted to know I'm sure."

"No, quite fascinating. Please continue Mr.—OK—Hobart," Heni said, responding to his smiling nod. Far different from the one he had given Ethel.

"Anyway, McClouds require extremely clean and cold water to survive, typically between fifty-five and sixty-five degrees. Crane Creek is right on the mark, spring-fed at fifty-eight degrees."

"Why the big, bad snakes, Hobart?"

"Don't really know as moccasins are generally associated with slower, warmer water. Could be that the watershed hosts so much of their natural prey? They supposedly lay in deep holes waiting for small critters to get close enough for them to pounce. They are big and scary, and I stay clear of them."

"What can you share about your lives together here along Crane Creek that our readers might find interesting or unusual?"

"Well, after spending the first part of our lives in Southern California, there could not have been a greater juxtaposition of lifestyles. Is that the right word, Heni?

"It's a great word, Hobart. Crane Creek is the polar opposite of where you spent half your life."

Hobart proceeded to share the joy and peace he and Ethel had found in their little farmhouse by Crane Creek for the next hour. At times they both leaked tears of joy for having taken the risk and made the move.

They laughed about Ethel's peculiar request to have treated water piped in from a nearby municipality, at "considerable expense" Elmer added, because of Ethel's irrational fear of creek-sourced water for domestic use. A condition of closing, so to speak, for the big city girl.

With the phone ringing in the background, Hobart headed to the kitchen.

"You handle the rest, Ethel, while I get the phone. I might be a while as I'm expecting a call from my brother in California."

"So, what can you add, Ethel? I am so grateful for you all sharing so personally. This is a beautiful story. Can you add your own take? What does Crane Creek mean to you?"

Ethel hesitated, then lowered her voice. "Do you really want to know, Heni? Magic is the word that comes to mind. But you can't share it with a soul, unless you are very close to someone who might benefit from what I say next. And, above all, you can't tell Hobart. I just feel that I owe it to others because of what Crane Creek has done for me. Will you promise me that? Only when this can be of critical use to another you love."

"I guess I can promise you that, Ethel. Please trust me."

Heni and Henry leaned in close to Ethel. She had already evidently survived the virus, so social distancing slipped into the shadows. Ten minutes later with ears ringing and eyes bulging, they leaned back to try and digest what Ethel had just shared with them. Her lifesaving dip in frigid Crane Creek.

"But, Ethel, the country, the world, needs to know this. If there is something in the waters of Crane Creek that knocks out the coronavirus on contact and some scientists can figure out what it is, millions of lives can be saved."

"You promised, Heni, and I took you at your word."

"But why, Ethel, why?"

"Because I promised Hobart. Maybe you can come back another time and ask him directly. Make something up about something that someone told you. Just don't tell him it was me."

"It looks like Hobart is going to be a while, Ethel, so we will be on our way. Thank you for an unbelievable day. We will touch base soon."

"Do you believe her, Henry? Was it just coincidence or did we just learn about a miracle cure for a devastating virus? And what do I do as a journalist when promises collide with humanity? You know that this is a blockbuster story, don't you, Henry? One that could make me, establish me, ground me in a career that is precarious?"

"And what if it is false? Nothing more than a big make-believe by a needy old lady?"

"I don't know, Henry. I usually have great trust in my instincts, but this one leaves me spinning."

"I understand, Heni. All I know is that Crane Creek has always been magical in my eyes, and I would put nothing beyond its reach."

chapter thirteen

THE VIRUS

ONE MORNING, ED AWAKENED FEELING AS BUM AS HE OFTEN ACTED. FIRST OF ALL, his attempts to come between Henrietta and Henry were getting no reaction. They seemed to just shrug off the inconveniences he had dumped on them and draw closer together. At this rate he would be inheriting a baby, as well as a girlfriend, even if he could break them apart. No, this was not working.

More importantly, he was coughing heavily, had a fever—though without a thermometer he couldn't be sure how high—and a scratchy throat. He was breathing heavily and with difficulty as well. Ed had watched enough TV over the past weeks to know what all of this added up to. Coronavirus.

Ed was young and healthy enough not to worry much about shaking it over time. At least that was his reasoning. No need to get too worked up unless things got really bad.

But a more sinister thought put a crinkly smile on his face. He had also read that the virus had a peculiar affinity for people of color. That Black folks had higher rates of infection, hospitalization, and mortality. Underlying conditions or something like that. And pregnant women had their own high-risk category. Black, pregnant, equals mortality. That was Heni. If what he had read and heard was accurate, she was extremely vulnerable to the worst that corona has to offer. If I can't have sexy Heni for my own, he reasoned, I can sure as hell make certain that idiot Henry can't, either.

Ed watched his potential victim's unit carefully the next twenty-four hours. And, sure enough, when opportunity presented, he was ready. It was early evening when he saw Heni kiss Henry goodbye, restore her mask to the proper place, and wave. He guessed that she was going to the neighborhood grocery store that they frequented almost daily. He would follow her wherever she led. It was the store, and he watched her athletic body carry her through the front door with forlorn lust. He then pulled his car up next to hers and exited, pulling a flimsy mask over his dripping nose and drooling mouth. Soon, he saw Heni pushing a cart back toward her car and intercepted her, asking if he could use the cart when she was finished. She nodded and opened the back hatch of her vehicle. As she leaned in to deposit a paper bag, Ed grabbed her arm with one hand and pushed her on her back into the rear compartment with the other. He then ripped the mask from her face, lowered his own, and open-mouth kissed her hard, smothering her surprised cries for help. A final spit cleared his throat. Having deposited all the saliva in his mouth into hers, he pulled his mask on again, jumped in his vehicle, and squealed off as Heni screamed for help. He spat through his window in departing, "It is not what goes into the mouth that defiles a person. . . ." Matthew 15:11

"I've been sexually assaulted," she sobbed to the two men rushing to help and trying to restore her mask to its prior place. She looked for the man who had accosted her but saw no one.

"Shall I call the police?" one of the men asked. "What did he do to you?"

"He forcibly kissed me. He tongued me. He spit in my mouth."

"That's sexual assault?" another asked.

"What else would you call it?" he responded. "Doubt that she was looking to get mouth-mugged in the grocery store parking lot in broad daylight. Makes no sense."

By this time, the store manager had made his way to Heni's vehicle, reaching for his cell to call the cops.

"Please don't," Heni begged. "I just want to go home."

"Do you know who accosted you? Did you recognize him. Did you get a good look at his face or his car?"

"No, no, and no. I'm OK. Just a little shocked and confused. Why would a complete stranger rip off my face mask, kiss me harshly, and not even touch me anywhere else?"

"I'm ringing the police."

"No, I'm going home. Now."

An hour later, Heni was snuggled in Henry's arms, trying to explain what had happened and understand why. Between sobs. It had been so fast and furious she simply hadn't registered any of the details."You didn't recognize him or his car?"

"No. I don't recall seeing either before. It is just such a blur."

"Tell me again about this kiss he laid on you."

"Well, he tongued me invasively. And then it was almost as if he spat in my mouth. It was all so ugly and gross."

"And he didn't touch you anywhere else? Only your mouth? What kind of sexual pervert is this?"

"And he shouted some Bible-sounding verse at me as he drove off."

"Bible verses and slobber? I just don't get it. Should I call the police, Heni? Report the incident? At least get a record going?"

"Why, Henry, why? What is there to report? A strange man, who I can't identify, did a strange thing to me, and sped off into the sunset before anyone, including me, knew what he was doing. Might make an interesting theme for a detective mystery but not in real life. Just hold me, Henry, just hold me."

chapter fourteen

THE FEVER

I T TOOK ALL OF SEVENTY-TWO HOURS FOR HENI TO START COUGHING AND SPIKE A FEVER. 102.6 degrees. She shook in bed when Henry tried to hold her. She was clearly exhibiting the prime symptoms of the coronavirus.

Henry called his doctor to request a test and, with his permission, drove her through one of the testing locations. They weren't necessarily surprised but still stunned when the results were positive. How could this be happening to them with all the precautions they had been taking?

The doctor prescribed Excedrin and a fourteen-day self-quarantine for both Heni and Henry. He did not feel it was necessary to hospitalize Heni because of her age and good health, and with Henry around to care for her, she should recover nicely. Henry needed to always wear a mask, separate himself physically, and slide food and drink through her door so he didn't get the virus too. And the baby should be OK, despite the recent addition of pregnant women to the "high-risk" category. Best to take precautions not to spread further he cautioned and call if breathing problems follow. Heni and Henry settled in for a season of recovery, still not comprehending exactly what had contributed to their dilemma.

Until several days later when a cheap bouquet of flowers arrived with a card inscribed, "If anyone sins and does what is forbidden in any of the Lord's commands, even though they do not know it, they are guilty and will be held responsible." (Leviticus 5:17)

Heni, still somewhat dazed and overheated at her now normal 102–103 degrees, could only shake her head in confusion.

Not Henry.

"The guy was trying to infect you, Heni, trying to kill you. The miserable son of a bitch did this on purpose."

"What, Henry?"

"The bastard who stuck his tongue down your throat passed corona to you. He is evidently some kind of religious fanatic and is gloating over our predicament. Sending flowers and Bible quotes. He knows where you live and where you shop. He tracked you down and infected you. Asshole! I bet he even lives close by. A neighbor? I wonder if he did all of that shit to your car? Or lent us his bedbugs?

"Why, Henry, why?"

"I don't know. Maybe because you are Black? Maybe because you are beautiful? Maybe because he is jealous of me?"

"Oh, Henry, I want to be done with corona. I don't want to infect you. I love you more than anything in the world, Henry. And our baby."

"Do you think you would recognize him if you saw him again, Heni? I could have the police scour our complex if you could provide a description? And maybe even get him in some sort of lineup for positive ID? This guy is crazy, and someone needs to stop him. Are you willing to meet with the cops and share this whole bizarre chain of events, including a description of the suspect?"

"I just can't, Henry. I don't have it in me just now. I feel horrible and weakened. I need to fight through this horrible virus and get better, for you and for the baby."

"For you, Heni."

"I want you to do something for me, Henry? I know it will sound odd to you, but I need you to take me to Crane Creek and let me lie in the cold waters, like Ethel did. I feel like I'm losing ground, and I don't want to go into the hospital with all of these other infected folks. And I can't stand to be away from you. Please, Henry, take me down there this afternoon. I promise that I will follow doctor's orders if this doesn't help. I promise."

"All right, Heni. I will do anything to make you feel better. And I will hold you to your promise if this doesn't work. Wrap yourself in a blanket, and I'll pull the car up."

Henry grabbed several towels and went out to pull the car up. He had wrapped Heni in a blanket and watched her wobble weakly from the front door toward him, finally picking her slim frame up in his arms and depositing her body into the back seat, where Heni lay down, clinging to her blanket and shivering.

"You are sure you want to lay your shivering body into a cold spring-fed stream and lay there seeking relief?"

"I'm sure, Henry," she stuttered through chattering teeth. "I'm sure."

Henry started the engine and headed south to Crane Creek.

Ed Jones looked on from the shadows of his front porch. A smile spread across his face. He had been watching them closely by day and night waiting for the virus to take over. It has worked, he thought with grim satisfaction. They are finally taking her to the hospital. His symptoms had abated, and he was well on the way to regaining his strength. His supposition that her presumed genetic weakness to the virus had proven valid. He hoped that she would never return. If he could not have her, no one could. He supposed that he would have to send more flowers to her memorial service and wondered what beautiful line or two from the Bible he could attach to close his case.

chapter fifteen

THE CREEK, AGAIN

"MR. CAMPBELL, IT'S ME HENRY HOARY AGAIN. MY GIRLFRIEND HENI HAS THE coronavirus, and she needs to visit with Mrs. Campbell again about Crane Creek ."

"She told you?"

"Where is the poor girl, Henry?" asked Ethel. "I think I can help."

"You promised, Ethel. No one but you and me."

"Saving a life, particularly a beautiful young one, is more important than keeping a promise, Hobart. Bring her to me, Henry."

"I don't want to infect, Mr. Campbell."

"He was around me for weeks and never even showed a symptom. Bring her in. Hobart, build a fire in the fireplace and get it roaring, just like you did for me."

"It's summer, Ethel."

"Build a fire, Hobart."

Henry carried Heni, still wrapped in her blanket, through the front door and to the fireplace. Henry unwrapped her nude body, which was shaking from fever and chills, laid the blanket on the ground, rewrapped her in a large towel, and nodded to Ethel.

"Tell him exactly how you did it, Hobart."

"Apart from forty years of age, your friend is the mirror image of Ethel when I thought I was going to lose her. She begged me to take her to the creek to cool her down to die, even though it was cold outside. I carried her down the hill to the pool of spring water and sank into it with her on my lap. Ironically, her first physical contact with the creek, ever. We both sat shivering, and I watched in amazement as her face transitioned from the flush of fever to the peace of relief and the cessation of a hacking cough. I sat for as long as I could, probably an hour or so, and finally, fearing hypothermia, rose and carried her back up the hill to the fire that was burning. I stoked it with wood and laid her in front, wrapped in a blanket. Her smile told me that a miracle had transpired."

"Henry, do exactly the same with Heni, and bring her back when you can't stand the cold anymore."

Henry hoisted towel-wrapped Heni into his arms, strode down the hill, and sat in the frigid water, with her submerged body cradled in his lap.

It didn't take long for him to see her fever flush turn back to beautiful ebony, and a slight smile creep over her face.

"Are you better, hon? You look it. Do you feel it at all? Can you tell any difference from when we first settled in?"

Heni nodded weakly, and then smiled more broadly.

"She's cured me, Henry, Crane Creek has cured me."

chapter sixteen

BELIEVE IT, OR NOT?

"**Y**OU WHAT, HENRIETTA? YOU HAD CORONAVIRUS, WERE HOSPITAL BOUND, NEXT TO death, jumped into some creek, and were cured? Just like that? And you are not the only one?"

"You need to get down here, Mr. Editor, and see for yourself. As soon as possible. And you can't tell a soul what I just shared with you. If you do, I will deny it all and leave you looking the fool."

"I will be there tomorrow morning, Heni, and I won't tell anyone. What's the address again?"

"It's a new one, and you should be happy that it is saving you rent expense on my behalf."

"You're living with someone, Heni?"

"Yes, and that's not all. But I think I should save a surprise or two for your arrival."

Ethel had helped towel off Heni before wrapping a blanket around her body. They had sat in front of Hobart's blazing fire for at least an hour. Heni with an aura of peace and tranquility about her, where there had been fever and chills just hours before. She looked into the fire as if in a trance. Henry, Ethel, and Hobart just looked, not sure how to comprehend what had just happened. No one would have believed it if the same hadn't happened to Ethel weeks before.

"I think I am ready to go home, Henry. Thank you, Mr. and Mrs. Campbell, for making it possible for my baby and me to survive the coronavirus. Thank you for sharing your story with us earlier, Ethel, or I never would have known to even try."

Hobart spoke first. "When Ethel told you, she said you promised not to tell another soul. Have you kept that promise, Heni?"

"Yes, I have, Hobart. Neither Henry nor I have told a soul."

"Well, I need to ask you to continue to keep that promise, Heni. First of all people will think we're crazy and have us see a shrink. Secondly, those who do believe you or are desperate enough to try anything, like drinking bleach as our stupid president blithely suggested, will descend on our paradise in droves, ruin our lives, and ultimately foul Crane Creek. I can't allow that to happen. I have a shotgun and a deer rifle at my disposal to provide protection."

"I'm sorry, Hobart, but I can't promise the same this time. There is too much at stake in terms of saving lives around the world. It would be selfish of us to hide a potential lifesaving cure at the expense of the millions of human beings at risk."

Hobart could only shake his head and slump his shoulders.

"What I can promise is that I will be discreet in revealing the magic of Crane Creek on corona. There is evidently something extremely unique in these waters that kills the coronavirus on contact. My quest will be to find out what that is and how to duplicate or extract it. My magazine has access to some of the most renowned scientists in the country, and the sooner I can get them sampling these waters, the more lives we can save."

Hobart could only shrug his agreement.

"It's the right thing to do, Hobart. I will start with the editor of my magazine, and we will develop a thorough and secret plan to pursue a cure and/or vaccine for the virus. He will want to see you and your creek, so please be available as soon as I can get him down here from St. Louis."

Hobart took Ethel's hand and muttered, "Our lives are about to change, dear."

"At least we still have lives to change, Hob. Too many don't."

Heni laid quietly in Henry's strong arms. She wanted to try and make love, but he rejected the notion, no matter how much he was longing for her.

"You're too weak, hon. It's too early. Let's not push our good fortune. When will your boss be here?"

"Don't know but definitely before noon."

The ringing doorbell dispelled that estimate. It was 9 a.m.

"Get the door, Henry, and I'll get dressed."

"Does Henrietta White live or reside or stay here on occasion?"

"Yes, sir, all of the above. My name is Henry Hoary, and I am Heni's fiancé. She's getting dressed as we speak and will be right out. Your name, please?"

"I am Heni's editor, Robert Winchell. I prefer Robert to Bob, please."

"Of course, Robert," Henry smiled, wondering in the back of his mind if this tall, handsome African American of the same vintage as Heni had been one of those past lovers she had listed as a failed relationship. In these strange times, anything was possible, he allowed. He would have to ask when the time was right.

"Coffee, Robert? You were up early this morning."

"Yes, please. Henry, it is?"

About that moment Heni burst from the bedroom and crossed quickly to Robert, putting her arms around his waist and kissing him lightly on the cheek. This hardly seemed a professional relationship. As he drew her into him, he suddenly leaned back from the baby bump he felt. "Is this your other surprise, Heni?"

"Yes, due in seven months. And you've already met Dad, I presume?"

Robert broke into a big grin and hugged her close. "Congratulations, Heni, I am so happy for you. Now, let's get down to corona business and the tall tale you shared with me on the phone."

Ed Jones was surprised by the surge of activity at Hoary's place. He expected a dejected Henry Hoary to return with his head down and a obituary to follow, with details of Heni's memorial service. Instead a strange Black man had shown up first thing in the morning, with Henry's car back in its normal slot. He hadn't heard him pull in the previous night but could only presume she must have gone quickly.

When Heni, Henry, and the Black dude emerged smiling and laughing later in the day to get into Henry's car, Ed gasped. Heni looked healthy and downright radiant. How could that be, he wondered. She had been on death's doorstep fewer than forty-eight hours earlier, and now she was the picture of vitality and energy. Now I really must have her, Ed thought to himself.

chapter seventeen

A PLAN

HENRY AND HENI DROVE ROBERT STRAIGHT TO CRANE CREEK, GIVING THE CAMPBELLS only a few hours' notice. It was long enough for Heni to share her miracle recovery with Robert, as well as that of Ethel. Robert looked more dumfounded than impressed.

"With God, Henry, Ethel, and Hobart as my witnesses, I was cured of a deadly positive case of coronavirus, with underlying conditions of race and pregnancy, from less than an hour of soaking in Crane Creek. You've got to believe me, Robert. And Ethel too. We couldn't make such stuff up."

Four hours later, Robert was a believer, albeit a reluctant one. And he was sitting on the story of a lifetime for his little magazine. The lines between professional journalism, fame and fortune, saving human lives, and keeping promises made were blurring.

Henry dropped Robert off at a nearby motel, awaited his check-in, and returned with him to meet Heni, who was preparing a simple meal of pasta, Italian sausage, and Caesar salad. The wine began to flow immediately.

"We've got to have a plan, gentlemen, a detailed road map if we are to protect the Campbells' privacy, research Crane Creek, find a vaccine or a cure, bring relief to millions, and be the first to break a blockbuster story," challenged Heni.

"I'm not sure that a plan consistent with each of these competing objectives can be crafted," offered Henry.

"We've got to try."

Four hours and two bottles of red later, they had at least agreed on one thing and had a grand old time getting there.

Robert had wanted to enlist the help of several scientists he knew of at Washington University to analyze the waters of Crane Creek and look for anomalies, in terms of chemical elements or properties. If anything showed up, he would draw a close circle of experts together to expand on their research.

Henry objected. He wanted to stay closer to home. Namely MSU, his alma mater and current place of employment. His reasoning belied his Mozarkian roots. He felt they needed to be dealing with someone or ones they could trust implicitly. That meant local to him.

He would take his former field zoology professor, a Dr. Turnbull, out for a beer or two, which is how he had passed the course years ago. He would seek his advice as to whom he might be able to put full confidence in to undertake some extremely important and time-sensitive preliminary research regarding stream qualities and chemistry. If Dr. Turnbull could provide no leads, they would go the Wash. U. route with Robert's contracts.

Most importantly, not one of them would mention a word about the true purpose of their shared mission to anyone.

Henry's inquiry could be done under the cover of a feature article his fiancée wished to run about a beautiful Ozarkian stream where cottonmouth snakes grew as big as an adult leg and rare West Coast transplanted McCloud trout had flourished and reproduced for centuries. Namely, Crane Creek.

Robert reluctantly consented, with some degree of confidence that they would end up back with his contact base ultimately. He just hated wasting any time.

Henry promised that he would contact his professor immediately, as time was clearly of the essence both in terms of potentially saving lives and breaking the story. Somehow, these humanitarian and economic ends, as at odds as they seemed, kept surfacing simultaneously. At least it was a start.

All three were exhausted when Robert, having started his day before sunrise, could simply not keep his eyes open any longer and slumped on the kitchen table.

Henry was in no condition to drive him back to the motel, and Heni suggested that he crash on their couch in the living room. He did, and she gently covered him in the blanket she had returned from Crane Creek wrapped in.

She crawled in close to Henry and snuggled up.

"I'm guessing that's not the first time you have invited Robert to stay for the night, is it?" Henry asked softly.

"No." She smiled back.

chapter eighteen

INQUIRY

HENRY INTRODUCED HENI TO DR. RICHARD TURNBULL AND RETREATED TO THE BAR for beers.

"Where does your interest in Crane Creek come from, young lady?"

"Just from reading about it in several periodicals. Pandemic stories are so depressing and repetitive I want to give my editor something refreshing."

"It is a beautiful and unusual place, Ms. White."

"Heni, please."

"Certainly, Heni, and thank you. Henry is a very lucky young man as far as I can tell. Anyway, a number of my graduate students do extended research on cottonmouth migration patterns in the immediate area of Crane Creek. The size of the snakes is unusual, even abnormal, if their behavior isn't. My students catch the snakes with large tongs, sedate them, implant microchips, and follow their movements over a year. Fortunately, no one has gotten bitten yet! I require them to sign a waiver protecting the university in the event that ever happens but still feel a personal responsibility toward each."

"I see you two are already into Crane Creek lore," interrupted Henry, plopping down a couple of Mother's Brewery Cobra Scares in front of them. Three beers later, they were still dancing. Dr. Turnbull couldn't figure out what it was that they were looking for. Neither could Henry nor Heni ascertain how to ask without revealing too much.

Henry finally broke the stalemate, guessing that Dr. Turnbull wouldn't remember enough after three beers at his age to draw conclusions.

"OK, Dr. Turnbull, we need a brilliant scientist to evaluate the chemical properties in Crane Creek, which might lead to giant snakes, reproducing non-native fishes, and other possible anomalies; isolate any abnormalities for subsequent research; do it quicker than quickly; and not tell a soul."

"Why, Henry? What's the rush? What's the secret? The creek has been here for millenniums and will be here tomorrow. Never mind. You won't tell me, and I won't ask more. I fear what you are seeking is well beyond my technical capacities, but I do have suggestion for you. You may consider this strange, but I think I know someone who can help you, if he chooses to."

"Sounds a bit unusual, but we don't have time to waste."

"Yes. He's an odd one, almost a pariah in the scientific community, who has left his past behind but not his brilliance. As an outcast, he operates under a pseudonym and is a much published and praised researcher and publisher of serious studies. Albeit anonymous. I only heard about him by chance through a personal friend, a Dr. William Thrush back East, who has worked with him on several highly complex projects. He sounds brilliant, and if anyone can fill your immediate need on a timely basis, it might be him. Again, if you can convince him of your cause, whatever it is."

"Is he local?"

"Sort of. Irving R. Randall, PhD, MD, Protem, Missouri, aka Dr. Arnold Coughman, professionally."

"Say what? I've heard of Protem but thought it was no more than a speck on the map."

"It's a long, convoluted story, if you have the interest and the time to hear it."

Thirty minutes later, Henry looked directly to Heni. "Guess we had better pay Dr. Randall a visit, as soon as possible."

"Thank you, Dr. Turnbull," he continued, "and please keep our conversation confidential. Any idea where we can find Dr. Randall once we get to Protem?" You wouldn't have an address or a phone number, would you?"

"Nope, but just ask around. Surely someone knows about an old hermit living on the outskirts of an excuse for a town, one who looks like death warmed over and avoids people like the pandemic. And, be careful. They still pack six-shooters down in Protem, I'm told."

"So, Robert is one of your past lovers, Heni? Sleeping with the boss?

Seems like a nice enough guy, a hell of a lot more handsome than me, and even the right color."

Robert was long gone back to St. Louis to await further feedback from Henry and Heni. They lay entangled in limbs and love.

"Stop it, Henry. Just a touch jealous? Well, you needn't be. First of all, he wasn't my boss when we were dating, and I'll ignore the 'right color' comment, which is racist, though, again, you likely didn't intend for it to be. I'll give you the benefit of doubt."

"I'm sorry, Heni, and I'm not jealous if you say I don't need to be. Just another typical stupid white man comment on matters of race that rubs wrong. How long did you date? Were you serious about him?"

"I suppose so at the time, but I felt it was inappropriate to continue when he did become my boss. I made the decision, he concurred, and we never looked back. And look what happened to me! Knocked up by my favorite man in the world!"

chapter nineteen

IRVING

RVING RANDALL, PHD, MD, NOW AGE SEVENTY-NINE OR SO, WAS BORN AN ONLY CHILD into an affluent and loving family in Bakersfield, California. He was surrounded by supportive parents with enormous vocabularies and given every advantage possible. His teachers also recognized his outsized intelligence early in life and recommended special accelerated schools to his parents. Irving graduated valedictorian of his private accelerated high school class at barely sixteen years of age. He completed a BS degree in zoology at Baylor University in two-and-a-half years and, in another eighteen months, had earned a master's degree in microbiology from Stanford. Twenty-eight months later, he had earned a PhD in molecular biology from Cornell University, in Ithaca, New York, where his doctoral dissertation is still displayed with pride by the institution as one of the groundbreaking contributions to that field in the twentieth century.

Still, Irving's thirst to learn more and more was not yet quenched, and his instincts told him to enroll in medical school to tie it all together. He graduated from Harvard Medical School four years later, with honors, of course, and with a new wife, Allison, an English literature professor he had met at Harvard. A two-year internship at Boston General Hospital was followed by three years of residency at John's Hopkins University, where, finally, everything he had learned and internalized blossomed into a fascination with the study of immunology. He had found his calling at last but needed yet more specialized training and study to compete at the top of his chosen field.

Cecil Atwater, PhD, MD, was an established icon in the scientific community, especially in the areas of microbiology and vaccine development. Over the years, he had successfully created revolutionary vaccine development approaches to several communicable diseases, including diphtheria, whooping cough, and hantavirus. He was leading a research team at Johns Hopkins University during the first attempts to develop an effective vaccine for the AIDS virus (HIV) in the early 80s when he took on Dr. Irving Randall, whom he considered a promising postdoctoral fellow, to assist him in the necessary research.

Following initial testing in rhesus monkeys for safety and efficacy, the Stage I and Stage II human trials on this trial vaccine for safety and efficacy on limited populations of human volunteers came and went with little fanfare or controversy. Unknown to his peers or even Irving, Dr. Atwater had substituted chimpanzee kidney cells for the original rhesus monkey kidney cells prescribed in the study for his cell cultures to grow Atwater's Modified Live HIV virus. It was a temporary question of access. Only his lab assistant of many years knew of this substitution.

Stage III of the vaccines trials was carried out using a population of 20,000 vaccinated volunteer subjects and 20,000 placebo subjects in double-blind fashion. The trials were proceeding nicely after six weeks' time, but the lab assistant suffered a sudden crisis of conscience and leaked the cell substitution information to a respected colleague at the National Institutes of Health. The story quickly took on a life of its own and finally made its way to the front page of the *New York Times*. After some investigation, it was discovered that Dr. Atwater's chimp cell cultures were contaminated with simian immunodeficiency virus, as well as two other chimpanzee pathogens thought to have zoonotic potential (transmissible from animals to man). Retribution by his colleagues and peers for this scientific heresy was swift and brutal. The Stage III trials were halted immediately, test vaccine supplies confiscated, and test subjects who received the virus referred for treatment to infectious disease experts, all at the expense of Johns Hopkins. These subjects were at risk, and their futures uncertain at best. Lawsuits flew quickly in all directions. The resulting scandal swiftly ended not only the career of the famous Dr. Atwater but also that of his research fellow, Dr. Randall, who knew nothing of the cell culture substitution.

It appeared that Irving Randall's career was over before it began. Though completely innocent of any wrongdoing or deception, he had been painted with the tainted brush that took down the King of the Hill, Cecil Atwater, and the scientific community, who had earlier welcomed a man of his elite academic credentials and obvious potential with open arms, now declared him guilty by association, a disgrace, a pariah, totally null and void. The hypocrisy and shallow allegiance of his former friends and colleagues was not lost on him, and he retreated as far from his previous academic circles as possible. A friend recommended the Southwest Missouri Ozarks, Mozarks, as being as remote philosophically, if not physically, as any place in the country. He designed and built a log cabin near the town of Protem that he and his wife settled in, embittered, angry, but mostly perplexed at how he had ended up in this position through no fault of his own.

Eighteen months later, being unable to live with Irving's bitterness and poor humor any longer, Allison left him for greener pastures. Both of Irving's parents died in a tragic car accident six months later, leaving him an inheritance of nearly 20 million dollars, which really didn't matter that much to him.

After two years alone in his cabin, drinking too much, grieving his beloved parents, and nursing his bitterness, Irving realized that his anger and disappointment was hurting no one but himself. He dusted off, purchased a powerful new high-octane computer, arranged for a sophisticated and very fast internet connection (not easily accomplished in Protem, Missouri), and set about renewing connections with several former colleagues in his field who had not dismissed him or bought into the lies about him. Years later, they would secretly refer to themselves as "The Gang of Five." He brought himself up to date on all of the relevant scientific literature in his field and those closely related to it and began to work in earnest again but now remotely and anonymously. He created a fictional curricula vita and a persona to go with it (passport, driver's license, social security card, beautifully forged but very convincing diplomas) and, with the support and encouragement of his network of loyal friends and colleagues, designed numerous studies that were published in prestigious refereed scientific journals under his new pseudonym, Dr. Arnold Coughman. He would even don a fake beard and blond wig when live remote computer consultations became necessary from time to time. Over a productive period of thirty years, Irving's "Gang of Five" had conducted numerous serious studies in the field of immunology and published over twenty-five articles in the most prestigious journals, with Dr. Arnold Coughman invariably the second author on all of them. If the National Institutes of Health only knew they were sponsoring and awarding grants to a phantom! As he got older, he realized that he was no longer a social person in any way and looked like hell most of the time. This bothered him only slightly on rare occasions, and he found that he actually enjoyed his anonymity and distance from the world more than he had initially realized. He was productive, making real contributions to his chosen field, and that was enough for Irving.

Dr. Irving R. Randall, PhD, MD, definitely warranted a visit from Henry and Heni as soon as humanly possible.

chapter twenty

GONE

"**S**HE'S GONE ROBERT, HENI IS GONE."

"What do you mean gone, Henry?"

"Just that. She went out to the store for a quick shop two hours ago, and hasn't returned yet. I drove up to see what was going on, and no one has seen her there today. Someone has taken her, Robert, I just know they have. There is more to the story of her getting the virus that we didn't share with you. This has got to be connected somehow."

"I'm headed down as soon as I hang up."

Heni had felt the knife point in her lower back, about baby level, before she smelled the fetid breath on her neck.

"Make any noise or look back and you and your baby are dead."

Someone or thing had jumped out from behind a large bush in Henry's front yard and now began to firmly push her down the sidewalk, knife urging her along. Soon a hand snaked out and slipped a pre-tied blindfold over her eyes.

"Why are you afraid, oh ye of little faith (Matthew 8:25–27)?" Heni's abductor mumbled in a gravelly voice.

"You will come with me to my humble abode, and we will make love. You have nothing to fear. In fact, I will bring you great pleasure. I will not force you for that would be rape, and I could be proven to have done it. No, I will simply keep you for as long as it takes for you to decide to have me of your own free will."

He gently pushed her through an opening door, pulled it shut it behind them, and led her to a straight-backed chair. He sat her in it and assured Heni that he had all of the patience in the world to allow her time to accept his kindly offer. "It is reported commonly that there is fornication among you (1 Corinthians 6:13)," Ed whispered.

Heni realized that the beast had not taken her far from Henry's. He must be a neighbor, the same Bible-spouting pervert who had planted the coronavirus in her mouth. Above all, she must keep her wits about her and find a way to escape. For her and her baby.

"You will come to see the wisdom of my ways, dear Henrietta, and welcome me into your arms. Until that time, if you become hungry or thirsty, just tell me and I will take care of you. If you need to use the toilet, I can help you with that as well. But I will not touch you until invited to do so."

"Pig."

"Oh no, lover to be, I am not a pig. And after you have experienced the pleasures I bring you, I will even give you the opportunity to stay with me rather than return to boring Henry. I am confident your decision will be a wise one. Until then, I must bind you to this chair and gag your mouth to give you time to come to your own conclusions."

"Pig. You are the one who attacked me at the store, forced the virus down my throat, and almost murdered me and my baby. You are the one who gave us the bedbug infestation. You are the one who damaged my car. You will never allow me to do anything of my own free will, pig."

"Enough, enough, beautiful Henrietta. You must mistake me for another. I have seen your beautiful body in all of its glory in Henry's backyard, and long for it. 'You are altogether beautiful, my darling; there is no flaw in you' (Song of Songs 4:7). I shall worship your striking beauty in the manner it deserves."

"Pig," she managed to spit out again before the gag could be applied.

After Henry had told Robert the whole story of sexual assault on Heni, the forcing of the virus into her mouth, the biblical quotes and references, Robert began to cry.

"You still love her, Robert," Henry sobbed.

"We both do, Henry, but she is yours now, and we must get her back."

They filed a report with the sheriff's department on a missing person. Heni was described as small, athletic, Black, and finally "beautiful" was mouthed by both simultaneously. They explained their relationships with her as fiancé and employer respectively but could offer no clues relating to Heni's disappearance or possible abductor(s) beyond the previous parking lot attack. An APB was issued, and Henry and Robert were sent home. Two days and nights passed without any signs of hope.

chapter twenty-one

A KNIFE

HENI POINTED TO HER GAG. ED REMOVED IT.

"OK, you are not a pig. I'm ready. You win. Untie my hands."

Ed untied her hands.

"I invite you to take me," Heni challenged as she slowly unbuttoned her blouse. "And take off this blindfold. I never sleep with a man whose eyes I can't look deeply into at moment of fulfillment."

Ed Jones removed the blindfold.

Heni blinked rapidly to try and adjust to the light she hadn't seen for days. As her captor's face came into focus, several things became obvious. He was the one who had forced the virus down her throat. She had never seen him before or after that attack. He wore a lustful leer.

"Do you have a name?"

"You can call me Ed."

For three full days and nights, Heni had desperately weighed her alternatives. Her abductor did exactly what he said he would. Nothing. But feed her, lead her to the bathroom, and sleep next to her, arms bound to the bedpost. Not once did he touch her inappropriately. Heni became convinced that his patience had no boundaries. He was not going to rape her. He would hold her and her baby in utero hostage until she submitted to his wishes. She had to do something.

Heni knew this man would kill her once he had her. She had no doubt about that. He was crazy, heartless, and cruel, in addition to patient.

She would have to see who he was before she could do anything else.

She would have to bluff her way into his confidence to have any chance at all of escaping. She would have to find a weapon of some sort to stop him. She would probably have to kill him or die trying.

Ed's voice was soft and cloying. "I'm glad you have come to see things my way, Henrietta. You hurt my feelings badly by calling me pig. I knew you would understand my genuine desire for you if given enough time."

"I'm sorry," Heni mumbled.

"It is God's will that you should be sanctified . . . that each of you should learn to control your own body in a way that is holy and honorable, (1 Thessalonians 4:3-4)," announced Ed proudly.

Heni knew she had to stall him. "How did you learn so much about the Bible? Your quotes and references are beyond common knowledge."

Ed smiled broadly. "Thank you, Henrietta. I have spent my whole life studying the most important recorded words in history. I am grateful you appreciate my efforts."

Ed took Heni's hand and led her to his bedroom. With her blouse gone, she had only bra, jeans, and panties remaining between her and this nightmare. She reasoned that if she allowed him to remove them, it would buy her a little more time and distraction. She knew at the end of the day, she would try and claw his eyes out if no other opportunity presented. She was prepared to die.

Ed laid her on his side of the bed and asked her to remove her clothing. Heni said she would prefer that he do it to add to their excitement. Ed bent over and unclasped and removed her bra, eyes aglow with lust. "Let her breasts fill you at all times with delight (Proverbs 5:19)," Ed shouted with abandon.

Heni forced a smile and whispered, "Talk dirty to me."

Ed was beyond self-control at this point. He removed the remaining articles of her clothing, each with a Bible verse accompaniment, of course. Heni and her baby bump lay naked beneath his hungry gaze.

As Ed removed his clothes, Heni reached her hands under his pillow to ready her fingers for attack. Suddenly, she felt something sharp. It had to be a knife. Probably the same one he had used on her. The son of a bitch slept with a knife under his pillow.

Heni clasped the handle. As Ed crawled on top of her, she drove the knife into his neck, twisted it, and stabbed twice again. Blood spurted everywhere as Ed gurgled and strangled on his own juices. Heni rolled him off her, wrapped herself in the bloody sheet beneath her, and raced to the door. She threw it open to emerge in bright sunshine, just several doors down from Henry's townhome, as she had suspected. A neighbor walking her dog screamed and ran. Heni walked calmly to Henry's front door and rang the bell.

As it opened, she threw herself into Henry's arms, sobbing loudly. "Heni, Heni, Heni—thank God. Heni, are you OK?"

Two hours later, Heni had scrubbed herself clean of Ed's blood and the shame of what had almost happened. She had shared her story with Henry and Robert, as well as the two deputy sheriffs who had been called to the scene by the frightened neighbor. Ed's body had been removed.

The deputies both seemed perplexed and agitated with her story. The white female deputy was particularly aggressive.

"So, Ms. White, you were abducted in full daylight by a man wielding a knife, held captive in his apartment for three days without being raped or physically harmed, simply because he wanted you to have sex with him voluntarily, which you finally agreed to do, and then stabbed him to death? And, furthermore, he spat in your mouth to intentionally give you the coronavirus? And probably did a whole bunch of other mean things from bedbugs to vandalizing your car? And you had never met or talked to this man before? Is this what you are asking us to believe, Ms. White? All of it?"

This set Henry off. "What do you mean? That you don't believe her?"

"Well, you have to admit that there are a whole lot of moving pieces to this murder."

"Pardon me, but it's not a murder. It is clearly self-defense against a crazy stalker and sexual predator."

"A man with no prior record, who attended church regularly, even taught Sunday School classes, and who is not here to give his side of the story."

"Get out of here now, and don't come back," screamed Henry, while Robert fought to restrain him.

The deputies looked at each other and left, promising that there would be more questions to answer. They also ordered her not to leave town, pending further investigation.

Once they were in their squad car, the skeptical deputy turned to her colleague. "How do we know she isn't some Black hooker named White, who shacked up with this dude for three days, and knifed him when she didn't get paid?"

Both chuckled out loud.

chapter twenty-two

POSTMORETM

HENI AND ROBERT TRIED TO CALM HENRY, WHO WAS BESIDE HIMSELF WITH ANGER. Heni had regained some semblance of stability, and the baby seemed unfazed.

"Are you really OK, Heni?" Robert asked.

"I think so. I've never killed a human before, but somehow it seems right to me. I had to protect our baby above all. And it was either us or him. Finding the knife when and where I did was nothing short of a miracle."

"I'm still not sure why you felt the need to take so much risk. Trying to scratch his eyes out seems nothing more than a shortcut to getting killed."

"I concluded that I really had no choice but to go for it. The creep wasn't about to do anything but wait. He had nothing better to do and was enjoying his little game. And I knew you all wouldn't have a clue where to find me. So, I went for it and got lucky."

"You are sure he didn't hurt you, Heni?"

"He didn't even touch me, except on the arm to guide me to the toilet. He even excused himself when I went. He fed me and gave me liquids. He was crazy, Henry. Crazy calm, crazy patient, and crazy per-verted. A stalker, yes, but more deeply crazed than any sex creep. The deputies obviously didn't seem to believe my story, and it does sound bizarre when you weave it all together. But it is all true. I don't know what else to tell them."

"You will tell them nothing more, Heni, except through an attorney," interjected Robert. "I know a damn good one who is a close friend in St. Louis, and I will speak to her tonight about next steps. That they didn't haul you into custody immediately means your story presents reasonable doubt as to any murder accusation. I'm sure the sheriff will be back. We will be ready. In the meantime, we've got to move forward with our Crane Creek plan as quickly as possible."

"I have a contact to follow up with, Robert, close to here, in Protem, Missouri. He is apparently a bit of a recluse and a rogue, but the real thing in terms of knowledge and credentials, according to my former MSU professor. We will pay him a visit as soon as Heni is cleared and feels up to it."

"You need to proceed with that visit, Henry, as soon as possible, to see if we are on to something that can be isolated and used to save lives. We have got to keep pushing. And Heni's back."

"Heni, we are so thankful you are OK," added Henry, holding her close. "Are you sure you are up to more chaos upon chaos?"

Heni teared up but nodded.

Somewhat surprisingly, further investigation from the sheriff's office never amounted to much. A visit from the sheriff himself didn't even warrant an attorney presence beyond phone monitoring. In fact, the sheriff seemed more irritated by the inconvenience of it all than suspicious or even curious. He didn't like deaths on his watch with the grisly follow-up that often followed. Particularly in an election year. Especially with all the mixed-race undercurrents, including the current boyfriend, the victim, and who knew who else. Throw in an unharmed baby in the accused's belly, apparently sired by the boyfriend, though he didn't ask, a purported COVID-19 case, and multiple accusations of victim malfeasance, and there simply were too many moving parts to try and piece together a solid case.

The accused had no prior record, a consistent if shaky alibi, and multiple character witnesses attesting to her professional and personal integrity. The forensics report he shared was pretty simple, death by stabbing, apparently in self-defense, and subsequent blood loss.

Maybe if he just thought on it some more, the whole thing would just go away. He did, and it did.

chapter twenty-three

A VISIT

HENRY AND HENI HEADED OUT SOON AFTER HENI'S TRAVEL RESTRICTIONS WERE lifted for Protem, Missouri. They took State Highway 125 and drove south toward the Arkansas border.

Henry had googled Protem the night before. It sounded like a strange place. Lots of history, most of it colorful, dating back to its founding in the 1870s. Even the name. When founders couldn't agree on what to call the town, they named it Protem. As one was quoted, "We'll call her Protem for now. That's Latin for 'just now.'" Unfortunately, neither his Latin nor his spelling of pro tem were correct, but Protem it remains yet today. Six hundred hardy hillbilly souls, two restaurants, one post office, and Highway 125 were about all that remained from the happier days gone by figured Henry. Shouldn't be too hard to find old Dr. Randall.

He read about Bank of Protem robberies, shootouts on main street even into the 1930s and 40s, and then a slow death spiral to the here and now, despite the proximity to the old White River, now a major lake destination, one of the last remaining operating ferries in the Mozarks, and beautiful Shoal Creek running through the village. In any even time still seems to be stuck in "Pro Tem."

One historical vignette had caught his eye. Seems some local ladies had a campaign to raise funds to put a new roof on the only church in town back in the 1940s. When completed, they celebrated with a church potluck social, at least until a couple of guys got into the "corn" and ended up shooting holes in the new roof. End story. Henry wondered if it was true.

"More than you ever wanted to know about Protem, right, Heni?"

Heni could only chuckle, for the first time in a while, and mutter, "Can't wait."

Their first stop was the old post office. It was old, really old, and though the town seemed to center around it, there wasn't much going on. An elderly lady was seated behind a counter.

"We're trying to find Dr. Irving Randall, and thought the post office might be a good place to start," offered Henry.

"Never heard of him," the lady said, not raising her gaze from the magazine she was reading.

Henry looked puzzled. Heni handed him the notes from their meeting with Dr. Turnbull. He scanned them quickly.

"How about Dr. Arnold Coughman?" Henry followed up.

"Oh, the crazy old coot who lives out in the woods and rarely ventures out? Sometimes wears fake beards and wigs like he's trying to fool someone? Why are you wanting to find him?" She finally looked up as if expecting an answer.

"Well, that sounds like who we are looking for. Can you tell us where he lives?"

"Go down 125 toward the lake, and take the second dirt track on your left. Follow it for a mile or so, and turn right into sort of a driveway, hidden by some trees. He'll find you."

The shotgun barrel stared down at them from the branches above. "What do you want?" A deep voice thundered forth.

"We're looking for Dr. Randall."

"He doesn't live here."

"How about Dr. Coughman?"

"Who sent you?"

"Dr. William Turnbull, Missouri State University. You don't know him, but he knows of you through your colleague, Dr. William Thrush."

"Bastard. Young whippersnapper Thrush, that is. He's not supposed to be dropping my name anywhere."

"I'm sorry."

"Don't be. Leave your car here and walk through the trees."

Randall carried a scowl on his face, was badly in need of a haircut and shave, disheveled hair pointing every which way. He was clad in pajama bottoms, slippers, and an old bathrobe covered in stains, with numerous holes in it. They followed him with trepidation.

Emerging from the thick clump of foliage, they both took a deep breath. Facing them was a hand-hewn log cabin, surrounded by forest, with a small, clear stream circling the perimeter of the cleared area.

"Come in," Randolph ordered.

Heni and Henry followed hesitantly.

While rough on the outside, the cabin interior had a comfortable feel, with a large river stone wood fireplace, a couple of wooden chairs, one small bedroom, and a loft. In the center of the living space were large tables holding three huge computer monitors and, below them on the floor, an enormous array of tower CPUs and storage devices. In other words, a computer geek's dream come true. Very few other comforts of home were visible at first glance, and it was abundantly clear that Dr. Randall's life revolved around his work.

"What do you want?"

"May we sit, sir?" Henry asked.

Randall nodded toward the two chairs and remained standing. Searing intelligence and barely concealed hostility blazed from his gray eyes with a suspicious glower that clearly dominated his every interaction with mere mortals.

"We need your help, Dr. Randall. All of humanity does."

He raised his eyebrows. "I'm aware of that, son, but what specifically are you asking for?"

"We have discovered a cure for the coronavirus, a natural antidote, so to speak. We need for you to help us isolate, produce, and distribute it fairly and equitably, without losing control of it to big money, corrupt governments, power, and greed."

"You know every great mind in creation is focused on that objective without the goody-goody conditioning at the end of your statement? What makes you think that you are better than all of them?"

"I'm a survivor, Dr. Randall," responded Heni softly. "And I know the reason why."

A long and animated conversation ensued.

chapter twenty-four

FIELD WORK

RANDALL'S CURIOSITY WAS PEEKED, AND HE BEGAN TO QUESTION HENRY AND HENI IN detail on what they knew, as well as what they suspected. They reluctantly shared their hesitation in revealing their discovery to anyone, including him, for fear of commercial exploitation. He agreed that they should be careful. Trusting him would be completely up to them, he observed. But he assumed that their presence spoke to that conclusion.

Heni nodded her concurrence and proceeded to share her story about contracting the virus, her sharp decline into medical oblivion, her request to be laid in the waters of a mysterious creek rumored to have healing qualities, and her immediate recovery.

Randall shook his head in disbelief. "You expect me to believe this malarky?" he spat at Heni.

Heni then revealed that she had learned of the healing powers from another, a lady in her midseventies who had contracted the virus. At the end, she had asked her husband to carry her out their back door to lie in the creek and die. Instead, she, too, had lived.

As Heni and Henry added details, Dr. Randall leaned in closer. He had never heard of Crane Creek, but then again he was hardly a local. Giant poisonous snakes and reproducing non-native fish triggered the zoology corner of his brain, and the abject naiveté of his visitors added credibility. The more they talked, the more deeply he listened.

He offered them bread and cheese for sustenance and apologized for not having more. They spent the night at Randall's cabin, huddled on the floor in front of a fire to keep the chill off, in lieu of wrapping up in one of his filthy blankets.

Next day, Randall began to raise questions they couldn't answer, technical questions about the creek itself, its watershed, and surrounding habitat. By midmorning, all agreed that their next action should be to take Dr. Randall to Crane Creek and let him have a look.

Besides, Heni and Henry were starving, and a fast food stop along the way would be most welcome.

Henry drove them all to Crane Creek, introduced Dr. Randall to Hobart and Ethel, then cut him loose with his collection equipment (jars, nets, etc.) to wade the creek and collect specimens for study, giving Henry an opportunity to explain who Dr. Randall was and what they hoped he could accomplish.

Randall returned to the older couple's house at nightfall and crankily declared that he had a close call with the largest cottonmouth snake he had ever seen. It was draped over his shoulder and had been shot in the head. No one was sure they liked that, even if in self-defense, but didn't question further. Dr. Randall obviously included a pistol in his collection equipment.

He also stated that he couldn't do it all in one afternoon, prompting Ethel to invite them for dinner and to spend the night, so Dr. Randall could get back at it first thing in the morning.

Specimens collected—including the giant cottonmouth and a small McCloud trout, labeled, and properly stored—they bid farewell to Ethel and Hobart by midafternoon of the next day and drove Dr. Randall back to his cabin in Protem.

On the nearly two-hour trip back to his cabin, Randall opened up to the kids, as he called them, about the many variables he had observed in one specific location that may be involved in the hypothesized healing effect of the waters.

For example, Dr. Randall had discovered a natural "hot spring" up one hillside above the creek. He had measured the temperature of the water at source to be 97.5 degrees Fahrenheit and concluded that it must ultimately flow into Crane Creek.

"How can that be?" asked a befuddled Henry. "Crane Creek is an exceptionally cold natural trout stream with an average temperature in the high fifty degree range. That's the only reason the McClouds can survive and reproduce."

"Fair question, Henry. My hypothesis is that the hot spring intermingles with several cold ones to cool it down along its way to the creek."

"Why is this even important?"

"I'll get to that, Henry, give me time."

Randall proceed to share his knowledge of karst topography with them, including large underground caverns, rivers that appear then disappear underground, and the typical chemicals and elements found there (carbonic acid forms, sulfates, sulfuric acid, and—including on rare occasions—soluble gypsum).

Hot springs and soluble gypsum? Henry's head was spinning. He didn't think he could process anything more until Randall blew it apart with his next observation.

Randall had read about a meteor storm, documented and known scientifically as the Weableau-Osceola event, that had taken place in the general area roughly 300 million years earlier. Meteors and astronomy in general, being another spare time hobby of his. Meteors often brought interesting and unusual things (including rare elements and molecules) to our planet.

Combine otherworldly elements from meteorites with extreme heat, a hot spring, and pressure, then add in the karst substrate natural chemistry, and who knows what could happen in this unique set of circumstances? The cottonmouth snake and McCloud trout blood draws amongst his samples might give up some clues.

Randall pledged to use all of his network of contacts and scientific resources, which he claimed included the best scientific minds of the day, many of them contractors associated with grants from the NIH, to help him find answers as quietly and quickly as possible. Randall liked these naïve kids in spite of themselves, and he admired their innocent altruistic spirit in such a damaged and cynical world as we inhabited today.

As the kids left Randall's cabin to head home, he warned them that this discovery process might take some time, perhaps as long as six months or more, as at least three different laboratories and teams would need to be involved.

"I don't think we have that long, Dr. Randall," challenged Heni. "People are dying around the world even as we speak."

"I can't promise anything, but you need to be patient, lay low, and keep your mouths shut. If my directed investigations do discover something of significance that indeed offers healing potential for the masses, then we will have the daunting task of bringing the substance in a usable, safe form to commercial production and wide distribution, while somehow avoiding the pitfalls involved in dealing with Big Government, Big Pharma, and world health organizations. I will move as quickly as possible."

Henry asked who would fund this no doubt very expensive investigation? With a wry smile, Dr. Randall offered that the researchers involved in the initial phases of discovery all owed him big-time favors and would be thrilled to be involved in an investigation of such significant potential import.

Henry and Heni were dumbstruck. In barely twenty-four hours, they had gone from nothing to most everything they could dream of. Robert wouldn't believe it.

chapter twenty-five

PANDEMIC, INDEED

O NLY THREE MONTHS LATER, TO THE DAY, DR. RANDALL SENT HENRY A CRYPTIC email with no details. He merely told him to get his young ass (and that of his far prettier coconspirator) up to Protem for a pow wow, ASAP.

Robert had been unhappy with the delay but intrigued by Dr. Randall's credentials and background. He would hold off on pursuing a similar course of action with his Washington University scientific brain trust.

In the meantime, people continued to get sick and die in the state, the country, and around the world. It had been twenty months since the coronavirus had surfaced in Hunglow, China. No vaccine, no cure, no antibody to effectively deal with the spread and devastation of the disease had been discovered.

Large pharmaceutical companies, small-venture-capital-funded start-ups, sovereign governments, spy agencies, and every other imaginable form of enterprise in between had bet millions of dollars on research, development, dry run production, and testing, only to find the coronavirus adapt and regenerate, always one mutation ahead of the many pursuers. No one had ever seen anything like it.

Herd immunity, or infection rates of 50–70 percent of a population sample, proved to be an ineffective deterrent due to high reinfection rates. Contracting the virus seemed to have no lasting effect on building antibodies to reject it beyond a month or two.

Undisclosed were the numbers of volunteers sickened or killed in the rush to be first to discover an effective vaccine. Controlling large-scale production and distribution would produce a financial windfall unprecedented in history and led greed to trump caution. As product was rushed to stage three testing without adequate proofs, safeguards, or protections, people lost their lives in numbers that would never be documented.

Equally as devastating were the side effects or lingering traumas for many recovering victims. Hearts, lungs, brains were repositories for virus remnants in many. Days, months, perhaps even years later, aches, pains, fog, listlessness, and general ill health would haunt some survivors. There simply hadn't been enough research to understand the whys and hows for some and not others.

A significant side effect of the failures to find a vaccine or a cure was the increasing unwillingness of many people to subject themselves to either. "Killed by the cure" became a rallying cry for rejecting interventions of any kind.

This virus had upset the world order as none before it and showed no signs of regression.

This was the state of the coronavirus world when Henry, Heni, and—with Randall's permission—Robert journeyed to Protem, Missouri, to hear what Dr. Randall had discovered and, more importantly, concluded about a Crane Creek sourced cure or vaccine.

chapter twenty-six

RESULTS

WHEN THEY ARRIVED, DR. RANDALL SEEMED DEEPLY AND GENUINELY EXCITED FOR the first time. They introduced Robert and explained his relationship, briefly surfacing a wariness between the two men, which quickly dissipated in the rush to share information.

Knowing their limited exposure to the fields of discussion he had to cover with them, Randall began to patiently and simply explain what his initial investigation had turned up and its significance.

It turned out that a necropsy or postmortem exam of the large cottonmouth had produced a couple of surprises. First, the snake had absolutely no internal parasites that could be detected, a pretty rare finding for a noncontrolled environment. This particular specimen of cottonmouth was at least twelve inches longer than the largest cottonmouth of record in the United States, and while it appeared to be an older snake in years, it had little to none of the aging pathological change that one would expect to see, such as kidney function deterioration, liver scarring, or CNS deterioration. The trout specimen showed much the same findings, again very unusual for the calculated age and size of the fish. Irving's working hypothesis? It appeared that some unknown factor present in the creek water was causing at least some of the local fauna to grow to greater-than-expected size, live longer than usual, and experience far fewer naturally occurring disease processes than expected.

Part of Randall's covert team's analysis of the water sample and other specimens had turned up an odd isotope (aluminum-26), which presented as an incidental finding when doing spectrographic analysis on the water specimen. This is an isotope not naturally found on earth but which is known to be abundant in our galaxy. Upon further analysis, it was determined that this isotope had bonded with at least three different organic compounds in the creek water, an unusual finding in and of itself, given what was known about its theoretical bonding properties and that it was revealing itself to be remarkably stable. The isotope exhibited a much slower-than-expected decay rate in that form, which to Randall's biochemist friends seemed truly bizarre and anomalous.

Randall emphasized that these initial results, though promising, were far from conclusive and that more robust testing of immune response to direct pathogen challenge was essential to their goal of deriving reliable and repeatable results.

That said, Dr. Randall knew that they were truly on to something important. Dr. Randall looked at the three sets of glazed-over eyes and broke into a smile before continuing.

To continue moving forward, he needed much more creek water with which to run further tests.

With Hobart's permission, and under cover of darkness, a team of trusted grad students was sent in a black, unmarked panel van to the creek once again, this time to collect much larger samples (220 gallons in all, in four chemically inert 55-gallon barrels) of the creek water from a location on the creek specified by Irving.

In Irving's lab, under his intense scrutiny, a highly concentrated, purified, and biocompatible solution of the organic compounds that contained specified quantities of the isotope (per unit volume) in a normal saline vehicle was developed over the following weeks.

In accordance with Dr. Randall's meticulous study design, the scientists exposed a total of eighty rhesus monkeys to the test solution and unmodified sterile water samples; Cohort One: twenty subjects by direct intramuscular injection (three injections of the concentrated solution once weekly over three weeks), and twenty more subjects (Cohort Two) by whole body immersion to the neck into a tank of the unmodified creek water sample for an hour's time, once weekly for three weeks. A third cohort of twenty test subjects was administered a specially prepared oral version of the creek water containing a specific concentration of the organic molecules containing the isotope. Finally, twenty unexposed monkeys (Cohort Four) served as a control group and were given sterile water only by mouth. The dosages, exposure times, and intervals of exposure were educated best guesses, based on prior studies conducted at their labs. A set of pre and postexposure laboratory, serology, and radiology studies were performed on all eighty monkeys four days before the onset of exposure and again two weeks following the last exposure.

The results gathered after six weeks of this rather primitive, hastily conducted initial experiment were dramatic, and totally unexpected:

Cohort One: No side effects were observed except mild redness at the injection site in three individuals. Postexposure Complete Blood Counts (CBC), urine analysis, and serum biochemistry results remained statistically unchanged. When postexposure antibody levels to six common viral rhesus pathogens were measured, however, the levels of circulating neutralizing antibody to all pathogens were off the charts in all but one of the subjects. The harder-to-measure T-cells of each individual were then evaluated, and the results were just as astounding. In all but one individual, T-cell populations were hugely increased over pre-exposure levels, as was their apparent functional activity. Radiographs of the thorax and abdomen (conducted pre- and postexposure) revealed significant (roughly 20 percent) enlargement of the spleen in all but one subject.

Cohort Two: Again, no side effects were observed in the immersed subjects, and no statistically significant change was noted in the blood/urine results from this group as a result of exposure to the unmodified creek water. Circulating antibody levels to the same tested pathogens as Cohort One were also increased in nineteen of the twenty monkeys this group but only by about half as much as in Cohort One subjects. T-cell activity and numbers showed a significant rise as well but, again, to only half the levels of those seen by the group that was injected with the test solution. No splenic enlargement was noted on the postexposure radiographic studies of the thorax and abdomen of these subjects.

Cohort Three: Side effects included vomiting post-administration in two subjects on one occasion and mild diarrhea in three subjects for two days post-administration of the oral solution. By the third day of trials, these symptoms had completely disappeared. Postexposure testing of this cohort revealed remarkably similar results to those of Cohort One, including unexpectedly elevated levels of neutralizing antibody to all six viral pathogens and marked elevation in numbers and functionality of T-cell populations. Radiographic studies revealed no significant organ enlargement.

Cohort Four (control)—No significant change was noted in any of these subjects related to blood/urine results, circulating antibody levels, T-cell activity, or organ size as measured radiographically.

The "how" of what had happened to the water in Crane Creek was less clear at this point than the "what" that had occurred. Under conditions unique to the topography surrounding the creek, a rare and heretofore previously unseen isotope (likely brought here in a meteorite shower) had somehow curiously and unexpectedly bonded with local organic compounds and become stable. Whether it was the superheated conditions of the mantle-driven hot springs or the heat combined with pressure or perhaps both of those combined with the presence of trace amounts of gypsum in that stew that had been the catalyst for this unusual bonding, he could not be sure. That was a subject for further experimentation at a later time. What Randall was sure of is that this rare chemical bonding had indeed taken place and that he could be relatively confident that the presence of these molecules in significant concentrations in this small creek was not coincidental to the fauna anomalies he had observed there. The inference of "healing properties" to the creek water was not as clear at this point but had him curious.

Randall repeated that these initial results were far from conclusive and that more robust testing of each animal's immune response to direct pathogen challenge was essential to their goal of deriving reliable and repeatable results.

He then patiently explained in detail the role that antibodies, B-cells, T-cells, and even primitive precursor immune system cells in the bone marrow play in our normal immune response to microbial invaders. He speculated that this enhanced T-cell function and the sheer numbers of them might account for the farmer's wife's rapid recovery when placed in the creek, assuming the source substance of the healing could be absorbed through the skin, which might very well be the case, at least to some degree, based on the experimental results so far. Even more remarkable, Randall told them, was what appeared to be some form of global or trained immunity in Cohorts One and Three.

He had read recently about the concept of "trained immunity" and tried his best to explain it in simple terms as an example of what they may be witnessing. Bottom line was that, inexplicably, sometimes being immunized with modified live virus pathogens (attenuated to lessen their virulence) resulted in immunity to more than just those specific viruses. Recent retrospective (backward-looking data analysis) studies suggested that there might be a relationship between highly vaccine-compliant populations (US Navy, City of Hong Kong) who had been immunized with the MMR (Measles, Mumps, Rubella) that had somehow developed an unexplained higher than expected resistance to the COVID-19 virus currently ravaging the world and, further, some apparent protection against the more deadly symptoms and complications of the disease.

What Irving's research was suggesting was that something similar might be happening after exposure to the creek water but, strangely, without the immune-stimulating properties of a viral pathogen to make it all happen. Strange, indeed, and very exciting! The results of this initial experiment had produced promising, if far-reaching, conclusions that demanded additional testing.

Dr. Randall couldn't be sure at this point, but it appeared as if direct injection of a purified sterile compound or oral administration might be the most effective routes of administration/exposure. Again, further trials to clarify were warranted, probably another six weeks' worth.

chapter twenty-seven

"WAIT A MINUTE"

"WAIT A MINUTE, DR. RANDALL," HENI INTERRUPTED. "HOLD ON. SIX MORE weeks of testing and then what? More tests? More deaths? To what end? Turn it all over to the CDC or the FDA or the WHO to study some more? You have already had a three-month initial investigation and six weeks of trial testing. And now you want six weeks more. When will it ever end?

"And your purified sterile compound injection. Who makes it? Who gets it? When? In what order of preference? The most vulnerable? The most important? The richest? Who even decides?

"I'm no scientist, but isn't what we are talking about here really pretty simple, if not easily explained? It's just creek water that, because of an interaction with some strange isotope, can cure this evil virus in young and old alike, as well as potentially introduce antibodies to ward it off to begin with and beyond.

"It would seem to be an immunity booster (read: vaccine) and a therapy (read: cure), all wrapped up in a single exposure to creek water. Ethel and I were cured by laying in it. You just need to prove ingestion works as well. How long can that take? You give a corona victim a glass and see if they get better. Same with protecting those exposed. A glass and see if they avoid infection. No specific dosage involved, just ingestion. Let's see if it's really magic. If it isn't, we go back to your protocols. If it is, we just make drinks of Crane Creek available to the world as soon as possible.

"I realize we need to make sure the water is safe to drink for everyone. I did an article about purified creek water once. I even tasted it. As I recall, it's pretty simple. You can add iodine or chlorine drops. You can run it through a water filter. You can dose it with ultraviolet rays. But easiest of all—you can simply boil it for fifteen minutes.

"I'm sure you are nervous about upsetting the delicate stew this isotope and this creek have created together. But heat, hot springs, are part of its equation. How can boiling it to purify change the balance?

"And who is at risk for any ill effect from purified water? Others, with wells or pumps along the creek, have been drinking it for years.

"I know the scientist in you wants to play it out by the rules, eliminate doubt and risk. God knows we wish others had done so. But what harm can come from giving away small bottles of purified Crane Creek water to anyone who wants to try it? No one is going to get sick from creek water that has been treated. The downside doesn't exist. The upside is simply humanitarian.

"More than two million people around the world have died of the virus in the last twenty months. How many are enough? When are we going to do something to save people's lives?"

Henrietta White was pacing back and forth, gesturing with her hands, eyes blazing, and going eyeball to eyeball with each of her male observers, before settling on Dr. Randall.

Randall sat in stunned silence. Robert and Henry stared at him, awaiting a response. His brow furrowed, and he sat motionless for at least five minutes before raising his eyes to Heni's and responding.

"You know, young lady, your logic is impeccable. I suppose someone could have a negative reaction to the chemical components of the water that extensive testing might foreshadow, but the risk seems minimal. I accept your theory and challenge. The problem becomes how do we get people, infected or not, to try it?"

"That's where Heni and I come in, Dr. Randall. We are reporters. We are writers. We have a magazine to distribute our stories. Our circulation is regional, but our story will attract other attention far beyond, particularly with Heni as case study. The world will know the secret of Crane Creek within weeks."

"Little shot glass bottles of Crane Creek Elixir can be available on call at a storefront in Springfield, Missouri, shortly thereafter," crowed Henry.

"Who is going to pay to produce and market these lifesaving little beauties?" asked Robert.

"I will."

All looked at Dr. Randall in stunned disbelief.

"But, first, you have to hook me up with a risk-taking local hospital administrator who can steer his or her existing and incoming cases and frontline care givers into a control group to sample our approach and provide rudimentary proof we can share with the rest of the world. It will be critical to our credibility. No more than thirty days at most, Heni, I promise.

"I know just the lady," offered Robert.

chapter twenty-eight

CHURNING

ROBERT WINCHELL HAD INTERVIEWED RACHEL ROBERTS ON NUMEROUS OCCASIONS. He had introduced her through his magazine to the St. Louis market as the new CEO of the third largest hospital system in a four-state area. Much to her delight and appreciation, he had told her story flawlessly and honestly, in contrast to much of the press who had picked at her youth, lack of medical credentialing, and relative inexperience. She was young for such responsibility, mid-thirties, but a proven, effective, and motivating leader. That she was beautiful, unattached, and not interested in being so only added to her mystic. She had invited Robert to join her for dinner several times, but it was only the product of mutual respect and desire to kick ideas around. They were good friends, and it was time to move the Crane Creek story out of the Mozarks and into a broader venue.

Robert had no problem getting in to see her in less than a week, purpose and honored guest unexplained, confidentiality guaranteed.

Robert trusted her on this one, even if the others weren't sure.

She sat listening quietly as Dr. Irving Randall began to speak in measured tones. She knew nothing of his controversial background, but Randall shared it all before presenting his case for a creek water-based coronavirus therapy and immunity booster. She was mesmerized by his intellect, knowledge, and familiarity with the nuances of the scientific community to which he anonymously belonged. He had even cleaned up a bit, shaved, and had his unruly head of gray hair trimmed and shaped by the Protem beauty salon lady.

Ms. Roberts interrupted Dr. Randall once to call her secretary, ask her to reschedule all of her afternoon appointments, and order in lunch for three. She listened in awe to the stories of Ethel and Heni, giant reptiles, meteor showers, and a tiny creek in Southwest Missouri that promised a cure for and protection against the deadly coronavirus. She later admitted that she probably would have shrugged it all off if her trusted friend and confidante Robert had not provided an endorsement. Lurking in the back of her mind was "what next?".

Dr. Randall's midafternoon ask was simple. He reached into the pocket of his moth-eaten sports jacket, pulled forth two small airline cocktail bottles filled with purified Crane Creek water, despite the Tito's Vodka label, and placed them on her desk. He opened one and slugged it down. "I will never get coronavirus. If you do likewise, neither will you."

CEO Rachel Roberts unscrewed the lid and lifted it to her lips, with a brief toast to the doctor, and sipped hers down more slowly.

"I told you she is a risk-taker, Dr. Randall."

"What I need from you, Ms. Roberts, is to be my partner, to serve briefly and confidentially as my sampling lab, to provide me with secret access to your most difficult cases and your frontline employees you can trust the most. It should take no longer that a month to produce a cohort of cured patients and immune staff. At which time your friend Robert will be prepared to share our secret with his readers and ultimately with the world. In short, you and select staff and patients need to become my laboratory, behind closed doors, beyond public scrutiny, for the next month.

"You might ask why and how I need only a month? The product, the one you just sampled, is no more than simple purified creek water that carries unusual chemical qualities, which stop the coronavirus in its tracks, after, during, and before contact, I believe. There is no risk to the participants, no need for FDA or other regulatory agency approval of purified natural creek water, no potential liability for your hospital system. Common people have been drinking treated water from Crane Creek for decades without suffering any ill effects. Standard testing protocols are not needed for this proven commodity. I share the source name with you with the confidence Robert has imbued in me about your trustworthiness. You are now one of only several people who knows. We must maintain the name and location of Crane Creek a secret to protect it and save it."

"Thank you, Dr. Randall. Your secret is safe with me," Ms. Roberts interrupted.

"The production and distribution of the Clear Creek Elixir, as we will call it, will be funded by private interests and provided to the public at no cost. With your help, within a month, we will have a story of cure and prevention of this indestructible virus that can begin saving lives immediately. I'm confident of it based on my research to date."

Rachel Roberts was speechless.

"What do you think, Ms. Roberts?"

She hesitated briefly, then nodded yes. "Count us in on the most important research project in history to date, Dr. Randall. I will pull together a small team of doctors and nurses whom I trust with my life and, with their help, segregate our sickest patients in confidential quarantine quarters. New cases will be directed there as well. No one need know that we are testing a new cure and vaccine for the virus, except them and me. Would you be willing to meet with them as soon as I can confirm individual participation? The story you share is so mind-boggling and compelling I want them to hear it.

"Sure."

Heni really didn't know where to begin. Robert had asked her to produce a cover story bombshell, single issue-oriented, all-encompassing exposé of the development of a cure for and prevention of the coronavirus that had taken over the world. She would include the results of Dr. Randall's hospital work as proof of performance as soon as available.

Robert had debated about whether to roll the story out in installments to drive more sales and revenues but, at Heni's urging, chose to go faster to save lives. They had also decided to keep the identity of Crane Creek secret, to protect Ethel and Hobart, and the near sacred waters from abuse and exploitation. No telling what a desperate world could do to a twenty-three mile stretch of pristine Ozarkian creek in hours if its identity were revealed.

She had thirty days to perfect her layout and copy, no photos included for fear of site disclosure, and prepare to introduce the world to Clear Creek Elixir. In terms of personal testimonials, only she, Dr. Randall, and CEO Rachel Roberts would be required to risk exposing their identities, in the interest of establishing credibility. Robert feared such exposure but felt it was necessary if anyone was to believe them and try the product.

These next thirty days would require a near superhuman effort to produce and ready product for market from everyone, not just Heni.

As an unsuspecting world awaited a magic potion, other researchers were competing frantically to be the first to market with a coronavirus vaccine. The financial rewards for winning this race were incalculable. Much was being done in secret. Some were closer than others, principally:

Pharma-Lax, Inc., a major international pharmaceutical conglomerate, had made their mark on the world, and huge sums of money, on patenting a pH sensitive laxative that adapted to individual body chemistries to eliminate the embarrassing side effects of gas and spontaneous eruptions produced by over-the-counter laxatives. They had also developed a prototype coronavirus vaccine that was being tested in secret on unsuspecting volunteers who believed they were part of a smoke cessation study. This was the third promising trial run for Pharma-Lax, with the previous two ending in the tragic loss of life from delayed allergic reactions. Scientists were confident they would reach product production stage within six months, complete with FDA approval. A special team of Pharma-Lax insiders, hand-selected by the CEO, had been assigned the tasks of keeping the scientists on point, monitoring competing projects, protecting the confidentiality of the process, being prepared to produce and distribute when cleared, and winning the race. At all cost. They had enormous power within the corporate shadow.

Glow Worm, LLC, was a start-up, venture capitalist-funded marketing company, which had hired an army of independent scientists, including former colleagues of Dr. Irving Randall, to spare no cost in developing a new vaccine, unlike any other in history. They, too, had tested in private, with some promising results that had fizzled when subjected to a broader sampling. Because of their nonpublic persona, very little was known about ownership or decision-making authorities and processes. Where power rested or how it was dispersed was a mystery. But their silence belied a competitive product.

The Republic of Petralux, newly renamed—a small, landlocked country—in Eastern Europe, was the first sovereign state to publicly announce a vaccine and begin testing it on government employees. Consistent with its closed-door and secretive society, little was shared about results or progress.

Petralux was believed to be sponsored and funded by Russia's SVR, successor to the KGB, and not much more information was expected unless or until they scored the win. With such backing, they were not to be trifled with.

There were others—corporate, private, and sovereign—slugging it out on the ground and behind closed doors. Yet nearly two years into a global pandemic, there remained little humanity could do to arrest the spread of the virus or save those most hard hit by it.

chapter twenty-nine

NEXT?

"**S**O, WHAT DO WE DO NOW?" BEGGED HENI.

She sat in a socially distanced conference room in CEO Roberts's hospital, with Dr. Randall, Henry, and Robert. A sobering silence filled the room just twenty-four hours after the elation of partnering with Rachel and her colleagues was shared among them.

Robert spoke first. "We're sitting on perhaps the greatest discovery the twenty-first century, a natural cure-all, which can lift the world out of its physical and economic death spiral. We've got to figure out how to confirm our product's effectiveness, how to mass-produce it, bring it to market, distribute it to the most in need first, explain its curative powers in simple but documented success terms, and do it in thirty days. With no regard to cost or profit."

"Sounds impossible to me," chimed in Dr. Randall. "I can do my part. I can confirm Crane Creek's curative powers in that time frame, if indeed my conclusions are correct, with Rachel and her staff's help. I don't have a clue about the rest. Except I'll pay for it."

Henry leaned back on his Mozarks roots again. "I think we ought to think locally and regionally as we roll it out and before dreaming about helping those most in need around the world. We can still prioritize on the basis of need in a smaller universe and perhaps subcontract distribution in larger, more diverse markets, so we are not perceived as playing God. Speaking of which, we need to avoid at all cost any inferences of religion or we will come across as fanatics and charlatans, as some promoters already have."

Heni rolled her eyes at Henry's tunnel vision but sensed that he was correct. At least they were going to do something!

"We need help," Robert began. "We need expertise, we need experience to even plan an approach. We need to form a team of experts whom we can trust to organize and produce a miracle while protecting our confidentiality. We have the scientific and medical expertise with Dr. Randall and Rachel, but it's my sense we need production, distribution, marketing, and legal consultation as soon as possible.

"I don't even know if we can legally take significant amounts of water out of Crane Creek, regardless of number of lives saved. Surely, there must be some restrictions? I have an attorney friend in St. Louis who can help keep us within the bounds of the law and advise as to whether we need to patent or legally protect anything. I'm not sure about the rest."

"You earned an MBA, didn't you, Robert?" asked Heni. "From prestigious Washington University, no less?" she teased. "Surely you know something about this stuff or at least whom we might invite into our circle?"

Robert shrugged and nodded. "All I know is to approach the MBA program director for suggestions as to how to access such expertise on a short-term basis and see what he comes back with."

Robert was in Dean Whipple's office the following morning. He ducked and weaved around the dean's most penetrating questions, before getting a couple of names and phone numbers. Dean Whipple assured Robert that each was trustworthy and beyond reproach when it came to confidentiality. He asked only that his business school be given proper credit for whatever venture Robert was involved in but not mentioned if it was a failure. Robert could only smile his concurrence.

Professor James Madison was a nationally renowned production process expert. Associate Professor Leonard Means was a specialist in logistics, namely how to bring product to market. Professor Lori Barnes had been Robert's adviser, given his marketing concentration, and his professor in several courses. She had given him As all along the way to graduation.

Robert decided that he would approach all three together rather than separately. They would have to work as a team if the professed objectives could be met, so they might as well flesh all that out up front. He was fortunate that all were available for coffee two days later, midmorning, and invited them to the hospital conference room. He asked Dr. Randall and CEO Roberts to join them.

"How do you know we can trust these guys, Robert?" Dr. Randall had asked haltingly. "It is imperative that none of this project gets out until we release. I not only fear losing a competitive advantage but possibly putting lives at risk. There are a lot of big players out there who would do anything to have what we have. A potential therapy and immunity booster, all wrapped up in one."

"I only know that the dean of the business school vouched personally for each of them, and I am known to or by several of them. Tell me where else to go, and I'm happy to try."

"Will have to do, I guess. Thanks, Robert," muttered Dr. Randall.

Dr. Randall spoke slowly and deliberately of the great hope he had in bringing forth a potent product to stamp out the coronavirus in human-kind forever. He revealed none of his background, research, or product sourcing. He spelled out a need for production, distribution, and marketing expertise to bring the product to market within thirty days and challenged each of the academics to be part of that moment in history. He promised more details in exchange for a short-term concentrated commitment of time and total confidentiality.

Professor Madison nodded his agreement that he could spare time from his fall semester teaching schedule for something so groundbreaking, subject to hearing the rest of the story.

Professor Barnes laughed and said she would commit, subject to Dr. Randall not telling her dean, lest she be assigned a larger course load.

Only Associate Professor Means was hesitant. He cited a publication he was currently working on in addition to classroom commitments. He asked for twenty-four hours to consider before formally committing.

Dr. Randall nodded his understanding and asked Professor Means to get back to him the next day. He then asked the other two if they had time for him to expand on his briefing that afternoon. Both agreed to resume after lunch.

"I need to talk to Deputy Smith as soon as possible."

"Who is calling?"

"I'd rather not say."

"You will or I will not connect you with him."

"OK, it's Means, Associate Professor Means, Washington University."

"He's on another line and shouldn't be long."

"I'll hold."

Two minutes later the following conversation ensued.

"What do you need, Means? You know I have asked you never call me on this number."

"It's important, Fred. It's about a meeting at a hospital I just attended."

"We're paying you a hell of a lot of money to research international product distribution, Means, not go to meetings at hospitals."

"But, Fred, someone is about to bust out a vaccine. Within thirty days. I only heard a summary report, but it was enough to convince me that they are serious and potentially capable. I have been asked to join their team and will do so with the intent of passing information to you. That said, you will have to pay me more."

The flow of critically ill patients into Dr. Randall's hospital test lab produced no surprises. Just verification. A glass of purified Crane Creek water eliminated their fevers, freed their congested chests to breathe easily again, and sent them into recovery immediately.

Administrator Roberts's medical staff was astounded. Several removed all protective gear, swallowed some purified water, and never looked back. Not a single one got the virus. Nor did anyone have a clue as to where the liquid came from.

Dr. Randall sent Henry back to Crane Creek for more water, arranged to have it boiled in large pots for a minimum of fifteen minutes, and cooled for administration in small doses. Hand to mouth would never work in the needy world, but it got them by in a hospital test environment.

The Clear Creek Elixir worked as forecast by Dr. Randall. A miracle cure was in the works.

chapter thirty

A START-UP

TWO DAYS LATER IN THE HOSPITAL CONFERENCE ROOM, ROBERT ROSE SLOWLY AND began quieting competing conversations.

"Welcome, all. I'm pleased to see that everyone is masked. That is the cardinal rule of the day any time we gather.

"We are here to start a new business with the express intent of losing money and saving lives. And we've got thirty days to deliver.

"Like any new business we need a business plan, complete with production, distribution, pricing, marketing, retailing, and expansion strategies. Scratch pricing, our product is free."

"You are our *team*, folks." Robert beamed. "Our corporate objective is to deliver a simple, safe cure for the coronavirus, which will serve as both an immunity booster (vaccine) and therapy (cure) simultaneously, at no charge, beginning locally and regionally with those most in need and expanding around the globe. We will work together to bring an end to the coronavirus on earth.

"Dr. Irving Randall will coordinate and confirm treatment and testing protocols and record the results in credible but understandable form.

"As you know may or may not know, our cure concept is keyed to a confidential regional water source. Attorney Lauren McCall will advise us on all matters related to relevant laws. Everything from who owns our water source, how much water we can withdraw at one time, and how the process is regulated to whether we need to patent or otherwise protect our natural product.

"Professor James Madison will organize and deliver a preliminary production capacity of X gallons of product, including transport from source to a treatment and bottling facility. He will focus his initial efforts on producing for a regional market, with a long-term plan to expand our reach beyond the region, even globally, while protecting the location of product source. Professor Madison is the only Wash U. team member with whom the location of sourcing shall be shared.

"Associate Professor Means will initially design distribution channels regionally and submit a long-term plan to expand nationally and internationally.

"Professor Barnes will develop a marketing plan for local-regional purposes only, assuming national and international demand will follow actual results.

"Hospital CEO Roberts will independently validate the results of Dr. Randall's testing program on her patients and staff and address them publicly.

"Henry Hoary will establish and manage retail outlets locally and regionally.

"I, Robert Winchell, will serve as general coordinator of this effort, focused on announcing and bringing Clear Creek Elixir to market in thirty days. I will utilize Heni White's blockbuster lead article in my regional magazine for the initial announcement. I will also record costs and disburse funds, generously supplied by an anonymous donor. We will meet three times a week, on Monday, Wednesday, and Saturday mornings at 7 a.m., to debrief and assess progress toward our mutually shared goals.

"Finally, Heni White will serve as our spiritual counselor, our conscience, our moral compass.

"This is the bare-bones statement of objectives and responsibilities, with each of us tasked with accomplishing our objectives by any means possible, without regard to cost.

"We will gather again this coming Wednesday to present individual pieces of our overall business plan and address challenges and problems each has encountered. I will synthesize your respective inputs into a draft business plan, which we will seek to approve in final form next Saturday.

"Are there any questions? Are there any doubts about our ability to do this?"

"I need to speak to Deputy Smith as soon as possible."
"Is this Means?"
"Yes."
"I'll put you right through."

"Our CEO has asked me to convene this emergency meeting of Team Pharma-Lax. As you know we were established to assure that our vaccine is approved and delivered to market before any competing product.

We have attempted to do this by pushing our own team of scientists and monitoring competition, among other things. We are instructed to win this race by any means available, and you will be compensated heavily for a win.

"We are meeting today because we evidently have a new competitor, previously unknown, but serious nonetheless. While we remain at least six months from delivering our vaccine to market, this one is on track to do so in less than thirty days and at no cost to recipients. We simply cannot allow this to happen.

"Thankfully, we have an inside source advising us frequently of who, how, and where they are progressing.

"At this point, the time frame is of more concern than the competing product. We will reconvene to plan action if needed, once additional reliable information is obtained."

"*Nyet*! Is not possible."

"I just heard it with my own ears. There is a potential coronavirus cure heading to market within thirty days, and it is not Pharma-Lax Inc's."

"What are they doing about it?"

"I'm not sure, but it won't be pretty."

"How can we get in on the action, comrade?"

chapter thirty-one

WATERS OF THE STATE

"**S**O, WHO OWNS CRANE CREEK, LAUREN?" ASKED ROBERT. "I THINK WE NEED TO GET this issue out of the way before any of the rest can make sense." The two were gathered alone in a confidential space.

"First and foremost," Lauren began, "water in a creek belongs to the people of the state, and public use of navigable streams is allowed. The land under a creek belongs to landholders adjacent to it, who, in turn, control access to the water from the bank. People may move upstream and downstream, i.e., canoe or swim, if they don't damage the adjacent properties.

"More specific to your question is the fact that Missouri is a riparian water law state. This translates into all landowners whose property touches or lies above a creek have a right to reasonable use of the water resource. This includes taking water for use on their property, if reasonable and doesn't deprive other landowners of their riparian rights."

"OK, this means that Ethel and Hobart need to be our conduit to the waters of Crane Creek and we can't drain her dry."

"In simplest terms, I suppose you are correct, Robert. There is a lot of gray area between your conclusions and mine.

"There is much confusion as regards regulatory authority. At the federal level, we've got everyone from the EPA to the US Army Corps of Engineers to the Department of the Interior through US Fish and Wildlife to the National Park Service to the US Forest Service to the president of the United States who appoints agency leadership.

"The state has its own Department of Natural Resources, the Missouri Clean Water Commission, and the Missouri Department of Conservation, each subject to their own political constituencies and lobbying interests.

"Point being, that innocent-sounding word *reasonable* that I mentioned previously has as many interpretations as interpreters. And then there is the vague notion of where the water removed is used.

"Bottom line? There are not a lot of specific regulations on removing water from Crane Creek. The only one I can find offhand relates to major water users, defined as taking 100,000 gallons a day, which do have to register with the state and submit an annual report on usage to the Department of Natural Resources."

"OK, I am confused now, Lauren. Just tell me what you think we can do with minimal public exposure and government—state or federal—regulation."

"I can't imagine we will remove enough Crane Creek water to even approach the reportable level, particularly in the beginning. And if Ethel and Hobart are on board, your access to water is assured. I understand that they own quite a bit of stream front, including that adjacent to the spring deemed so important by Dr. Randall. Less clear is whether we actually have to boil the water on their property to comply with their riparian rights."

"I guess we need to visit with Hobart and Ethel as soon as possible. What will we need legally from them, Lauren?"

"I would suggest an easement, permanent if they are willing, that will allow us to access the creek from their land and either remove it for processing or construct a rudimentary processing and bottling facility on their land. All you are talking about is boiling and bottling, correct? Guess we will have to see what Professor Madison comes up with before getting more specific."

"Correct. I'll grab Heni and Henry and try to get down to see them tomorrow afternoon. Can you draft something up for me to review with them? I think we need this assurance before our Saturday planning meeting. We can present it as our intention tomorrow morning."

"I'll see what I can do."

chapter thirty-two

PROGRESS

ROBERT CALLED THE SATURDAY MORNING MEETING TO ORDER AND PASSED AROUND copies of a document marked "TOP SECRET" on the cover, just above "Draft Business Plan for Clear Creek Elixir." Getting there had been timely but not easy.

At Wednesday's meeting, each leader had discussed their preliminary findings and ideas. Robert suggested that they talk about the water first, in that everything else revolved around that.

Attorney Lauren McCall briefed the leadership team on her conclusions regarding ownership of source water. She confirmed that it was in Missouri, without mentioning the name or locale of the creek. She explained that state law is crystal clear. The people of Missouri own the waters of the creek. The people of Missouri own the raw material for an immunity booster and a therapy to rid the world of corona.

That said, landowners along the creek have riparian rights that entitle them to reasonable use of the water as long as it doesn't infringe on other landowners' rights to same.

"It is my conclusion that if the landowners, who are known to us, will sign an easement granting access to creek water on our behalf, within the confines of Missouri law, we can do so. I have prepared such a document, and we will be speaking to the landowners soon. It is less clear that they can grant us the right to remove the water from their property, but I believe that is a risk worth taking, subject to what Professor Madison has contrived in terms of production. For purposes of today's discussion, I believe you can assume that the landowners will agree and that we can proceed with each of your plans."

Robert thanked Lauren and asked Dr. Randall and Rachel Roberts for an update as to the effectiveness of the purified creek water in curing sick patients and preventing frontline workers from infection.

Dr. Randall confirmed a 96 percent cure rate and no worker infections during the testing period to date. Ms. Roberts nodded her concurrence. "The Clean Creek Elixir works. Without doubt. The sick keep pouring in and leaving healthy. Their relatives are starting to wonder why and how."

"OK, we have a product that works and access to the raw material that makes it so," confirmed Robert. "How do we produce it and bring it to market? Dr. Madison, your thoughts, please? Please keep it as simple as possible, so all of us can understand your basic concept."

Dr. James Madison believed that a simple stainless steel tank boiling the raw creek water for at least fifteen minutes would provide adequate purification to protect consumers.

"Springfield is blessed to be called home by several of the leading manufacturers of such equipment for the wine and beer industries.

"Let's say initially we purchase a used 20,000-gallon stainless steel vertical heating tank. Fairly expensive, but you say cost is not a consideration.

"We can rent a small warehouse to house the tank and related bottling line. Then we hire a hauler to pump 11,600 gallons of creek water per day into a fifty-three-foot liquid tank trailer. Both are the maximum capacity allowed by interstate law without special permitting, which we need to avoid.

"Is there a minimum dosage size required to attain these remarkable cure and prevention rates, Dr. Randall?"

"There doesn't seem to be, Professor Madison. We have experimented with everything from a four-ounce glass to a tablespoon full of liquid and have seen no measurable differences in outcome."

"Good," continued the professor. "Because for purposes of my production line example, I'm using 1.7 oz. mini liquor bottles, airline shooters or nips as they are commonly referred to, to estimate production capacity output based on the tank trailer referenced above.

"Given the formula of 128 ounces in a gallon, divided by 1.7 ounces to produce seventy-five doses per gallon, our 11,600-gallon-capacity tank trailer would allow us to produce and bottle 875,000 doses of Clear Creek Elixir daily in the small 1.7 ounce minis for distribution in large cardboard boxes.

"The bottling and boxing technologies are widely available. They've been doing it for decades, just without the magic ingredient. Think whatever brand of spring water you saw last week on the grocery store shelves. No doubt branded as healthy and good for you, 'pure Ozark spring water,' and the like. Little do they know just how good.

"With this initial investment we will have established the capacity to produce over 6 million doses per week, considerably more than we need locally or even regionally, and more than enough to get us on the map and expand distribution.

"Provided these assumptions are correct, we can dose close to 25 million citizens per month, or 300 million citizens of the US per year, with just one tanker truck and half of a stainless steel tank. This is just short of our national population of 330 million. All in one year.

"But let's think bigger. Suppose we make three tanker deliveries a day instead of one or purify 35,000 gallons of Clear Creek water in two 20,000-gallon stainless steel tanks daily? We essentially triple our production capacity to 2,625,000 doses per day; 18,000,000 doses per week; 75,000,000 doses per month; and nearly 1,000,000,000 doses per year. We can essentially inoculate the entire population of the United States of America in four-and-a-half months and begin to think and plan globally. What do you think?"

There was stunned silence around the room. They hadn't even gotten to distribution, marketing, and retailing yet, and the reality of a widely deliverable deterrent to and cure for the coronavirus had been translated into a realistic model.

Heni raised her hand. "What about the creek? Taking 11,000, or even 35,000, gallons of water out won't effect it or the species who reside in it?"

"Funny you should ask, Ms. White. I consulted a stream hydrologist friend with the same question. He simply laughed at me. He explained that a very conservative estimate of headwaters flow on Clear Creek in all but periods of severe drought is 5 cubic feet per second. In that there are 7.5 gallons in a cubic foot, that equates to 37.5 gallons of flow per second; 2,250 gallons per minute; 135,000 gallons per hour; and 3,240,000 gallons per day. If we extracted 35,000 gallons per day, it amounts to barely 1 percent of daily flow at very conservative levels. At normal rates of daily flow, the impact is negligible. Dare I say, drop in the bucket?

"Looking at it another way, the state's largest spring averages 300 million gallons of flow per day. Not 3,000,000 like our little creek. 300 million. Bennett Spring on the Niangua River just north of Springfield averages 120 million gallons a day. There's nothing like that on our creek, but just think how many significant springs keep it flowing steadily and cold through the seasons. If we are careful with our withdrawal procedures and don't impact the riparian corridor, which protects the creek, the effect will be miniscule. I do fear what others might try to do if they got wind of it, which is why we need to keep its location top secret, forever."

"Regardless of where the water source is located, how do we keep from drawing attention to it with three tanker trucks going back and forth daily where once there were none?" asked Henry.

"Excellent question, Henry. I don't have a ready answer, but I'm confident that, by varying routes and times of mobility, we can avoid detection. We simply have to. Any other questions before I yield the floor?"

"So, is what you have just reported really possible?" questioned a slightly skeptical Robert Winchell.

"Check my math out, Robert, and draw your own conclusions."

Dr. Irving Randall could not suppress the smile on his face.

Dr. Means's and Dr. Barnes's reports were of a broader nature but spoke to the clear compatibility of distribution and marketing the elixir with production capacity. Henry envisioned storefront locations locally and regionally initially, giving away the elixir as a sole product. He noted that they would be creating jobs in communities hard hit by the virus as well as saving lives.

Heni reported that she had begun to draft her blockbuster magazine bombshell and was confident she would have a draft available for the team within week.

Robert promised to condense these strategies into a concise professional business plan to be handed out and questioned Saturday, before a final vote of acceptance the following Monday. It would guide their actions and deliberations for the next three weeks.

"Less than one week in, we are right on schedule in terms of meeting Dr. Randall's promise of one-month delivery to market. It is critical that we keep this progress and these plans to ourselves."

The first order of business Saturday morning was a report from Lauren about meeting with the property owners. Would they make access to the creek water available to us for a long-term basis? Lauren referred the group to Appendix A of the business plan for the answer. It was an easement agreement executed by the Campbells that did just that for ten years without restriction, with their names redacted.

What was not shared was that they were also changing their will to pass ownership of their property to Heni and Henry Hoary at the time of their deaths and subject to the couple being married.

"This will assure that the farm and access to the creek will be granted for the foreseeable future."

Rachel Roberts asked why they couldn't go ahead and approve the plan as written this very day. Everyone knew what was in it and to waste a weekend of their tight schedule made little sense.

Robert asked the team how they felt about moving forward. A collective nod provided an answer.

"OK, if so, are there any other questions to be raised before we vote?"

"Do we need to patent Clear Creek Elixir?"

"How can one place a patent on a purely natural resource that is owned by the citizens of Missouri?" responded Lauren McCall.

"Good point, Counselor."

"When and how do we involve the United States government in our process?" asked Professor Barnes.

"Never. As far as I'm concerned, they had their chance to provide structure and leadership to coordinate a national response to a deadly global pandemic, and they did nothing. Look what we will do in thirty days. In terms of coordinating communication and distribution with other countries, we may need an assist from the State Department. But above all, we cannot politicize this product or access to it. We do not need the federal government's approval to give away purified creek water and will proceed with product introduction on our own, utilizing the press, conservative and liberal, to earn credibility. Robert and Heni will manage that process, after we have gone public. This is our product, our gift to a suffering world, and we are in charge."

The speaker was Dr. Irving Randall.

"Are we moving too quickly?" wondered Rachel Roberts. "It all seems so simple."

"It is," affirmed Heni, delighted that her early pleas for expediency had been heeded. "The product is simple, the process is simple, and the objective—saving lives—is simple. And noble."

Saturday's vote was unanimous. The draft "Draft Business Plan for Clear Creek Elixir" was no longer a draft. It was the real deal.

A ragtag bunch of quasi professionals had stumbled onto a miracle cure and deterrent for the deadly coronavirus and was preparing to share it with the world at large.

chapter thirty-three

OBSTACLES

I T HADN'T TAKEN LONG FOR THE NEWLY APPROVED BUSINESS PLAN TO FALL INTO competing hands.

"This is Means, and I need to talk to Deputy Smith as soon as possible."

"One moment, please."

"What do you have, Means?"

"I've got their whole plan of production and distribution of a cure for and deterrent of the coronavirus, in great detail. They are intent on getting a bottled purified creek water product into stand-alone dispensaries locally within three weeks."

"You mean like Poland Springs or Ozarka or some hokey commercial product? Who in their right mind could believe that it will cure or prevent coronavirus? Who will pay for it?"

"It's free."

"OK, it's still the wackiest idea I've ever heard of. And we've done some research on this guy Randall whom you mentioned last visit. He is a renegade, a pariah in the scientific community. He was implicated in fraudulent testing protocols decades ago and has been an outcast ever since. He has no credibility with any scientists, domestic or international, of good standing."

"Well, he's the one driving the bus and claims to have a near perfect cure rate in a secret hospital clinic with this purified spring water over the past several weeks. As well as no new infections among frontline unmasked providers."

"Do you have any idea where he's getting the water or how to access it?"

"No, he has confided only in Professor Madison, who is designing the production process. Randall, the two young ones who seem to have discovered the creek's purported healing powers, the attorney, and the magazine publisher Winchell—who is kind of shepherding the whole process—are the only ones in the know.

"So, if you had to take one of them out to dramatically alter their progress, who would it be?"

"Hmmm. I didn't know the doc's checkered past. That surprises me. He seems so professional, so intelligent, so knowledgeable, so confident. I suppose you could use that major blemish against him and the product when they release and not have to hurt anyone?"

"I do not, repeat, do not want a product on the market before ours."

"Then, I guess it would have to be him."

"Bring that business plan to me immediately."

"When will I get paid?"

"As soon as we determine whether this is a real threat to our product and timing or not."

At the emergency team meeting for Pharma-Lax, Inc., later that day, Deputy Smith shared Associate Professor Means's verbal input and handed out copies of the written report Means had provided.

"I want each of you to review this business plan in detail and be prepared by tomorrow morning to opine as to whether you think it has any merit or possibility of success. The idea itself makes no sense to me. Purified creek water to bring a global pandemic to its knees? Come on. But I need your help. Each of you seven brings a unique perspective to this discussion, which is the most important one we will ever have, so be thorough and honest. We will gather at 10 a.m. right here to decide next steps. It has been suggested that Dr. Randall, who has very questionable credibility in the scientific community, be taken out. I need to know your views on that as well."

"Comrade, I have just left a secret Pharma-Lax meeting where the new competitor's plans to bring a product to market, in three weeks now, were shared with my team, along with their business plan detailing specific strategies."

"The Republic of Petralux, through my agency, will pay heavily for such a document. Our vaccine testing process is coming along nicely, but we can't compete with that schedule, let alone be assured to beat your company's product to market."

"I figured as much and can transmit it to you immediately upon receipt of the agreed-upon funds. But please know the whole idea seems ludicrous. Bottled purified creek water from some unknown source that serves both as a deterrent to and cure for the virus to be provided through stand-alone retail outlets for free? Are you sure you want to pay a substantial sum of money for that information?"

"A transfer will be effected immediately to your personal account. What do you think Pharma-Lax, Inc, is going to do?'

"We still seem to be focused on delaying the process through eliminating one of their key people, probably the scientist who is leading the testing protocols. Our team of scientists seems confident that we can produce an effective vaccine, which will make our company a shitload of money through sales to sovereign governments if we can just be the first to market. We could care less about a cure at this point. Only a vaccine."

"I haven't read your document. Although it does seem to provide a laughable conclusion, what if it is real? What if they really have discovered a cure and a vaccine in this mysterious water source?"

"You mentioned in a previous conversation a young pregnant lady whom they refer to as their spiritual leader?"

"Yes, she is profiled in the business plan with other members of their team. In fact, she appears to be the one who discovered the magic waters and claims to have been cured of the virus by laying in them. She also is apparently the one pushing hardest for early release of the product and free distribution, to save lives, of course."

"Obviously, a very idealistic young lady."

"Indeed. If you could grab her and hold her for ransom, namely the product source, your country could conceivably gain a significant competitive advantage in bringing, and selling, a broad-spectrum product to market. There could be considerable financial windfall in that. And, surely, this band of crazies would not let their spiritual leader and her unborn baby dangle helplessly in harm's way?"

"Just what I am thinking. Can you provide information on where to find her and plan an abduction?"

"I should be able to do so after tomorrow, as I'm sure we will be reviewing the logistics involved with taking out one of their leaders. I'll send what I have today and touch base tomorrow."

"So, why are you working with us to win this race and not your own organization?"

"You are paying me more."

"*Harasho*, comrade."

chapter thirty-four

A PRODUCTION LINE IN PROCESS

I N THE MEANTIME, PROFESSOR MADISON SET OUT IMMEDIATELY TO ACQUIRE A USED stainless steel tank from a local producer with an international following, while Henry researched available rental warehouse space, preferable in locally remote locations. Madison pulled in a colleague from a bottling plant and, without revealing the nature of his product, offered him a substantial consulting fee if he could assemble a primitive production line for "bottled" water in less than a month. His colleague wasn't sure but said he would try.

Dr. Randall kept administering the elixir to virus-laden patients, curing literally each one of them and sending them home. He also pulled out his checkbook to fund creation of a bottled water production line.

Heni worked feverishly on her Clear Creek Elixir exposé while Robert began to prepare an initial press release distribution list. He canceled the Monday and Wednesday meetings since the business plan was in place and his team had work to do.

Others pursued their respective objectives vigorously, except for Associate Professor Means, who had other ends to meet.

Team Pharma-Lax met as scheduled and decided three important things:

    – The bottled creek water scheme was bizarre and unlikely to prove legitimate.

    – However in the interest of absolute caution, it was imperative that production and distribution of Clear Creek Elixir be disrupted immediately.

    – The easiest and quickest way to do so would be to assassinate Dr. Randall.

They heavily debated whether a smear campaign keyed to his previous misdoings could undermine his product enough to make it laughable and avoid bloodshed. In the end, the entire team was obsessed enough about being first to market and the financial rewards that went with it that they took the "easy" way out. Deputy Smith had access to the shadowy world of hired hit men from his time in government and would proceed immediately. Randall was living in a cheap rundown St. Louis hotel with other key colleagues near his "test" hospital site. He would be easy to isolate. This would stop their upstart competition dead in its tracks.

The COO of Pharma-Lax, Inc., signed off on every aspect of the operation. Their product must and would be the first to market, cleared by authorities for immediate production and distribution keyed to their thorough testing protocols.

Dr. Irving Randall was feeling fully at peace with himself for the first time since he had been tragically smeared and professionally ruined decades earlier. His brilliant works under an alias had afforded him some redemption, at least in regard to his abilities and intellect. But this was different. He was actually doing something to immediately impact humankind, something he had dreamed of in those early energizing and inspiring days of his career. This was what he was created for, educated to do, and destined to deliver.

He walked crisply in the settling dusk toward his hotel room, where he and those of his colleagues who wished would gather appropriately distanced with open windows inhaling the cool fall air for wine and takeout food before preparing for another grueling day of pushing and pulling. As far as Randall could tell, everything was proceeding as scheduled, and in his case, the near perfect cure rate had extended yet another day.

For reasons he could never later explain, Dr. Irving Randall felt a compulsion to leap his nearly eighty-year-old body skyward and thrust his fists into the air. He did so just as a shot rang out from his left, bullet striking him midsection instead of mid-chest.

"Shit," the gunman muttered, gunning his car into escape mode.

He was passed by a streaking ambulance blaring its siren, headed toward Heni and Henry's hotel room. Her water had broken prematurely, and their baby was at risk.

Heni's SVR sponsored abductors looked at each other in disbelief as Heni was wheeled out on a gurney, sobbing about the baby, with Henry trailing directly and desperately behind.

They had previously staked out the couple in the hotel based on information provided by the Pharma-Lax informant and approached them in the lobby to ask about a rumored cure for corona that was being studied in a local hospital. They had heard about it from officials in their government and had been dispatched to find out more.

Some young lady named Henrietta White had been mentioned as one who had benefited directly from a waterborne cure. They wondered if either Heni or Henry knew anything about her or it.Heni and Henry stared at each other in disbelief. How could these total strangers who presented as Eastern Europeans in accent and dress know anything about Clear Creek Elixir?Henry regained his composure and shrugged lightly. "Never heard of such a thing or person, but we could sure use a cure for the virus, couldn't we?"

"Indeed. I was wondering if we could buy you all a drink and visit about how or who we might follow up with. We are total strangers to this place, and any help you could offer would be much appreciated."

"Would love to, but we are headed back to our room for room service. As you can see, my wife is expecting soon and, as such, in a high-risk category for infection from the virus. We avoid all trafficked areas."

"We will be fully masked up as we are now if that makes any difference."

"No. Sorry. Good luck with your quest, it is certainly a noble cause," offered Henry in parting.

As soon as the elevator doors closed, Heni burst into tears. "How could they know all that, particularly my name, as total strangers representing a foreign government? We've got to let Robert know as soon as possible that someone is snooping around and may have the goods on us."

"First thing tomorrow, hon, first thing in the morning."

Anticipating rejection, Heni's abductors had obtained a master hotel key from a desk clerk in exchange for a large sum of cash. They had planned to hang out in the lobby until the bar closed, then slip into Heni's hotel room, disable her roommate, and abscond with her to a Republic of Petralux safe place in the country, a ransom note left behind. It would offer her safe return in exchange for a bottle of Clear Creek Elixir and directions to product source. Otherwise, she and her baby would be killed within forty-eight hours. Instructions on completing the exchange would be provided via a message left on her cell phone by morning.

It had been a brilliant plan, now to no avail. They would stand down to await further instructions.

Ironically, Irving Randall and Henrietta White arrived within fifteen minutes of each other at Rachel Robert's hospital, both in the ER, neither aware of the other's presence. Small world, indeed.

"Someone knows what we are up to," growled Robert Winchell to Rachel Roberts early next morning. "But, first, how are the patients?"

chapter thirty-five

DEEP BREATHS

"**T**AKE A DEEP BREATH, ROBERT."

Rachel reached out and grabbed Robert's hand. She squeezed it gently. They were seated across from each other in front of her desk.

"Both of our colleagues are in trouble. We delivered Heni's baby by C-section, and while very small, she seems to be reasonably healthy. Heni is struggling. She hemorrhaged heavily, and we are scrambling to build our supply of her rare blood type. She is hanging on in the ICU. We will have to keep the infant as well, pending her recovery."

"How about Dr. Randall?"

"Dr. Randall is in critical condition. This was likely an assassination attempt gone wrong. A single shot entered through his pelvic area, severing his spinal cord at base, wreaking havoc on his digestive system. His age is a major complicating factor. I can't tell you if he will make it, but if he does, he will be crippled forever.

"He asked that a message be delivered to me during one of his brief moments of consciousness. I need to call Dr. William Thrush, phone number in his briefcase. Thrush will know how to proceed in Dr. Randall's absence, as they have evidently been in regular contact about our product. At least that is how the message was relayed to me. Short story? Dr. Randall is at grave risk."

"He'll make it. He's a tough old bird."

"And there is more, Robert. Henry tried to explain a strange encounter he and Heni experienced last evening before their rush to the hospital, which is all the more frightening in the shadow of Dr. Randall's shooting. It involved two foreign nationals, the use of her name, and the mention of a secret corona curing potion. Henry was in and out of coherency, and I had trouble keeping him focused. He said he would explain this morning and literally begged me to keep them both safe."

"When can I see them, and what do we do now, Rachel?" Robert asked, glancing down at their still intertwined hands. Her soft smile belied a deeper emotion.

"He what?" shouted the Pharma-Lax CEO. "He missed the doctor? He only wounded him?"

"Yes, sir," responded Deputy Smith. "He claims the target moved suddenly as he fired, and his single shot struck him in the midsection. The doc was taken to the nearest hospital, which happens to be the one where he is conducting his secret clinical trials. No idea about his condition or whether he will survive."

"At least he's off the frontlines for now. That should slow them down. Let's take a deep breath and keep pushing our product to market."

"She what, comrade? She went into labor before you could grab her? Where is she now? In the hospital with her premature baby?

"And the Pharma-Lax hit on the doctor was off target? And they are both in the same hospital? Could this get any more bizarre?"

"Do you wish that we continue our efforts to grab her and negotiate a swap?"

"No. Their whole concept seems cockamamie enough without taking additional undue risk to steal it. Tell your Pharma-Lax source to keep sharing what his informant leaks to them, and we'll breathe deeply and keep pushing our trials."

"This is what we do, Robert. I'll pull Henry in to elaborate on his strange tale and will contact Dr. Thrush about joining us as soon as possible. We'll need to pull everyone together immediately and explain everything that has happened. We all are likely at risk from some unknown assailants.

"I also worry about a leaker in our midst but am not sure how to flush him or her out. It is critical that we maintain our momentum. I will check the status of Dr. Randall and Heni and arrange for you to visit as soon as they seem stable enough. That should take care of today.

"Perhaps, most importantly, we take a deep breath and have dinner at my place tonight."

A PUSH

ROBERT CONVENED HIS SHOCKED TEAM IN EMERGENCY STYLE, MASKS IN PLACE, EARLY the following morning. It had taken most of a day to round them all up, given their respective frantic levels of activity. They sat in front of him stone-still, full of rumors and concerns.

Robert reported the probable assassination attempt on Dr. Randall, Heni's premature delivery, and the security intrusion attempt by two Eastern European actors. All in one day.

Henry confirmed that both mother and baby were in relatively safe zones. Rachel shared that Dr. Randall was in imminent danger, having received critical wounds to his spinal cord and internal organs. Henry shared the details of his hotel lobby exchange. Then Robert questioned whether someone was leaking information from the team. An uneasy murmur spread through the room, with glances to and fro.

"The risks associated with our endeavor have clearly escalated. If anyone is uneasy, now is the time to step aside."

Dr. James Madison spoke up loudly. "All of this is immensely troubling, but the idea that someone is betraying our confidence and sharing our secrets is devastating. Robert, I demand that you go around this room and directly ask each of us if we have spoken or shared information outside of our circle."

"All right, Professor Madison."

After eliciting the expected denials from all present, Robert observed that only Heni and Dr. Randall were not on the record yet, but since they both were victims, they were beyond suspicion.

"That said, I do know that both of these corona warriors would implore us to carry on, per our original schedule," challenged Robert. "Dr. Thrush, whom Dr. Randall referred us to, will join us by late afternoon tomorrow to oversee the testing protocols in Rachel's hospital. I doubt that we will lose much momentum there during this transition. One upside to his engagement is the immense credibility he enjoys in the scientific community, which was one thing, as Dr. Randall shared with you early on, that he had stolen from him as a youth. With Dr. Thrush's endorsement and involvement, the results generated from both treatment and prevention efforts over these past several weeks carry immense weight. I know that if he survives, Dr. Randall will want to fight his way back into the mix as soon as possible, and Rachel's staff will work toward that end. But Dr. Thrush will lead us forward on the medical front in the interim."

"What about Heni?" questioned Professor Barnes. "We need her. She is living proof that the elixir works, and her blockbuster article was the intended launchpad to the world. She's now a seriously impaired mother with a premature baby during these next critical weeks. Who is going to fill that void? That piece is at the heart of my preliminary marketing plan."

Robert hesitated briefly before turning to Rachel Roberts with a soft smile. "Heni has a rough draft of the magazine issue nearly complete, including interviews with the anonymous survivor and herself fully fleshed out. I intend to ask Ms. Roberts to step in and pull Heni's work together for publication. I will assist her along the way. We will have something to you, Professor Barnes, within the week to incorporate into your marketing plan."

"As for everyone else, please keep pushing forward. Production line, Professor Madison. Regional distribution, Professor Means. Documentation of water easement and successor trustee, Ms. McCall. Warehouse for production facility and a couple of storefront distribution points, Henry.

"We have only two-and-a-half weeks to meet Dr. Randall's schedule, folks, and sadly I am certain that he will not be back in the mix before that window closes. I will report to all daily on the condition of our fallen colleagues and will schedule another get-together to meet with Dr. Thrush as soon as he is settled in. "There is no denying that we have entered a dangerous phase of this project. Someone wanted to stop Dr. Randall. Having not stopped us, it is likely that they will try something else. I don't know how they obtained information on us but can only trust each of you to maintain full confidentiality of our status at this point. Please be careful, travel in pairs if you can, and report anything suspicious to Rachel or me immediately. We will share a full progress report from and with everyone at next Monday's leadership meeting. Any questions?"

Rachel lingered behind as Robert sat contemplating his self-imposed timeline.

"So, are you going to help me bring Heni's draft to completion, Rachel? Sorry I didn't have a chance to ask you ahead of time."

"It all depends, Robert, on whether we get to pick up where we left off last night?"

Robert rose and took Rachel into his arms. They kissed fiercely for a moment before Rachel broke away.

"See you at 6:30, Robert Winchell. Don't plan on going home this time."

"I am so thankful that you and the baby are OK, Heni. All I can think of is protecting you and little Emma, not saving the world. Are you still OK with that name? Emma Marie. Your mother's name and that of mine?"

"Yes," Heni responded weakly, still struggling regain her bearings. "It's a beautiful name for a beautiful young lady. I'm still too weak to pump breast milk for her but better than yesterday."

"She's in good hands, Heni, not to worry. Just get your strength back and the rest will follow."

"Henry, I need to get my draft article polished into final form. How am I going to do that?"

"Robert has asked Rachel Roberts to work on it with him. I know they will keep you in the loop. Again, not to worry, Heni. It is in good hands."

"Did you talk about the guys in the lobby who confronted us with insider information? And who might be responsible for a leak?"

"Yes and no. We discussed the exchange in detail, but apart from going around the room and confirming everyone's commitment to confidentiality, it was kind of left dangling. I'm not so sure that those guys were not out to bring harm to us, as well, the more I've thought about it."

"Maybe they were just messaging, letting us know that they are on to us? To try and scare us back into our hole?"

"I don't know. That they knew of you by name scares the hell out of me. Look what they did to Dr. Randall. He is barely alive."

"You think they knew it was me who they were asking about?"

"Yes."

"So, who do you think is collaborating with them?"

"I don't know, but I have never had a good sense of what Associate Professor Means is up to. He hasn't produced one concrete idea yet nor evidenced what he is working on. He's kind of aloof and removed, more observer than actor. Someone is definitely putting us and our initiative at risk, and I'm going to share my concerns about Means with Robert tomorrow."

"Be careful, Henry."

"No, you be careful, love. They know your name and story."

"So, how has one so beautiful as you avoided the marriage trap, Ms. Rachel?"

"I think I could ask the same of you, Mr. Robert."

They lay close and found themselves feeling even closer.

"Surely, you've had serious suitors over the years."

"A few."

"Is that all? You are just going to leave me hanging as to how many, for how long, and how important to you?"

"In my case, Robert, the 'hows' are better left untouched. I can share that I have admired you since I first met you back when and felt an underlying attraction. I'm happy to finally have acted on it and find the outcome genuine and exciting. I hope you have as well?"

"I think the answer to that is fairly obvious, given what's playing out beneath these sheets."

"Stop it, Robert. Were you ever married or engaged?"

"I guess the only way I'm ever going to find out more about you is to share more with you about me. Never married but close once. Ms. Heni White and I once had a real thing for each other."

"Wow" was all Rachel could respond. "What happened?"

"Well, I was promoted to be her boss. She loved her job, and she felt it was inappropriate for us to be serious lovers in such a situation. So, she broke it off and has done great work for me and the magazine ever since."

"She chose her career over you, and you just accepted it?"

"Yes. Surely you have had career choices that conflicted with personal ones throughout your meteoric rise through the medical hierarchy. Did you ever fall in love with a doc?"

"I don't think I've ever really been in love, Robert. I was a bit of a wild thing in my younger years. I guess I viewed shared intimacy as a toy of sorts, to be played with and grown out of. I never stopped to challenge my view. I hope you don't think less of me now."

"You used the word genuine a few moments ago. Do you really feel that?"

"Yes, Robert, I do. But enough for now. Who do you think is leaking? To have that much information, to know the whereabouts of our key people, to even know Heni by name is way beyond coincidence. Someone is flushing all of our information, including our business plan, most likely, to someone else who is desperate enough to kill to stop us. How can we stop the hemorrhaging before another is hurt? We've got to do something quickly."

"I don't know, Rachel, but I agree with your conclusions."

"For some reason, I don't trust the Means guy."

"Robert, I need to talk to you. It's about Professor Means. Can I stop by?"

"Sure, I'm here all morning."

Minutes later, Henry was in Robert's small office. "Heni and I think Professor Means is cheating on us. We don't know how or with whom, but we can do without him."

"Funny thing, Rachel agrees with you and Heni."

chapter thirty-seven

A RECKONING

"I NEED TO TALK TO DEPUTY SMITH, IMMEDIATELY."

"Means?"

"Yes."

"One moment, please."

"Means?"

"Yes, sir. I'm afraid they are on to me. The botched efforts of the past two days to intimidate and derail their efforts have only heightened their resolve. They have a new scientist on board to cover for Randall if or until he heals. And who in the hell turned loose the guys with the foreign accents, asking about Heni White and curative water? They know there is a leak, and I sense they suspect me. I denied, along with everyone else at our emergency meeting, but this guy Henry's gaze never broke from me. Finally, Winchell has asked me to meet with him first thing tomorrow morning. What do I do?"

"We need to get you out of there without hesitation, Means. I think you are at grave risk for exposure or harm. Stay in your room. Call in sick or something. I will arrange for a pickup within twenty-four hours. Above all, don't talk to any of them. And be assured, Means, your feedback has been invaluable."

"I agree, Deputy Smith, we need to take him out. He knows entirely too much. None of our involvement can ever see the light of day. You have my approval to proceed with another hit, just please find someone who can shoot straight this time."

"I think we will just disappear him. No blood, no guts, just missing in action."

"Means just called in sick, Robert. He left a message and said he would let us know when he is feeling better. He promised to have his regional distribution plan ready for presentation at our Monday meeting."

"Interesting, because I just scheduled an appointment for tomorrow morning to confront him over your concerns, Rachel. Henry and Heni share them as well. They think he is the leak. If I get even a sense of deception from him, he will be relieved of his role immediately. Let me know when he calls back."

"And about tonight, Robert? Same time, same place?"

"You aren't getting tired of me yet, Rachel?"

"Au contraire, just getting started."

"OK, Means. At precisely 2:00 this afternoon, a blue Buick sedan will pull up to your hotel entrance. Don't wait in the lobby, just walk straight from your room through the front door and get in the back seat. You will be delivered to a safe place, debriefed, and sheltered until this whole corona mess is nothing but ancient history and we are all wealthy."

"Yes, sir."

"Means has disappeared, Robert. I sent one of my aides over to check on him late this afternoon, and he was nowhere to be found. No one at the hotel saw him leave, but his room was cleaned out. There is no doubt that he has been funneling our plans directly to someone, likely a competing source of vaccine, in an effort to keep us from bringing Clear Creek Elixir to market. He has probably shared his copy of our business plan with them, as well, so they know everything about us. What do we do now?"

"At least we are rid of him. Crane Creek is not mentioned in the plan, and he was never privy to its name or location, although he and they now know it is in Missouri. Depending on whether it is a large corporation, a foreign government, or even an agency of our own country, they are likely scouring the state for a potential source as we sit here. And, then again, maybe not. Who knows what we are dealing with? We just need to keep our heads down and move forward."

"Comrade, our insider is gone. I'm not at liberty to share why or how, just that we have no one feeding us information any more. I'm not sure what that does to your planning process."

"What will Pharma-Lax do now?"

"Our team has been told that we will shift our focus to a massive, multi-million-dollar campaign to discredit Dr. Randall. We will drag out all of the dirty laundry related to his original sin and blanket the world with it. We have dozens of scientists who can cripple his credibility and impugn his morality. We will have our attacks ready to unleash at the moment of their big announcement. Cheap bottled water produced by a deadbeat, washed-up liar will not be given a chance to take hold, free or not. And we can conjure up all kinds of risks associated with a barely tested therapy of such a spurious nature, as well as promise a thoroughly vetted and tested vaccine within several months. Why would anyone choose risk and expediency over certainty and safety? It just doesn't make sense."

"Interesting."

"Incidentally, your guys with the foreign accents dropping names and confidential information really put everyone on alert. Not sure why you did it that way."

"It was SVR leadership's decision. They wanted to come across as insiders in the hope of gaining credibility with the targets and easing access to the girl."

"Well, it didn't work, comrade. I believe we are leery of further engagement with these loonies and really at this point remain pretty skeptical about their prospects. We will proceed with our product and engage in character rather than physical assassination. We cannot risk being labeled a party to any sabotage. I know that this is a different tone than we were spouting even as recently as a week ago, but it is coming from the top. More to lose than gain or something like that. What about the Republic of Petralux? What next for you all?"

"Do you think the young guy, Henry, I think it is, is worth grabbing? I'm interested in your read on his value and influence."

"Well, he is evidently one of only a few people who know the source of their 'magic product.' We have a dozen operatives out scouring all of the creeks in the state, trying to look for I-don't-even-know-what. They all look, smell, and feel the same. I doubt that anything will come of it. I honestly don't know if his barter value approaches that of a young pregnant lady but not much to lose. Just be a little more subtle this time, please. You are giving all of us a bad name. That said, I've enjoyed working with you and wish you guys well in your efforts to broker a deal."

"You have been worth every ounce of currency we have spent on you, and I will miss our collaborations. Who knows? If you get any more insider information you feel we could use, the price is still right."

chapter thirty-eight

REBOOT

"**I**RVING RANDALL, YOU LOOK TERRIBLE."

"Well, dodging an assassination attempt at age eighty tends to rattle one's rafters. I am so glad you are here, Dr. William Thrush, my friend. You are the only one who knows enough to keep our momentum going, and you bring a hell of a lot more credibility to our product release than I ever could."

"I am impressed with the team you have assembled. Sidebar, up front. This Robert Winchell seems driven and organized. Does he have something going on with the hospital CEO?"

"Not that I know of, but I've been out of the loop for a while. Just as long as it doesn't distract him."

"On the contrary, they seem to be a well-functioning leadership team."

"A team, huh? That is a little different dynamic than before."

"How are you feeling, Irving?"

"Not good, and the prognosis is stark."

"I heard. I'm so sorry."

"It is likely I will never be able to walk again and will be wearing a colostomy bag for the remainder of my years. Frankly, if it were not for waiting to see the good done by Clear Creek Elixir, I'm not sure I would want to carry on. Still near perfect recovery and prevention rates in our little test unit, William?"

"Yes, it is utterly amazing. You all have a real game changer on a global scale if we can get it out."

"Why do you think someone shot me, William? A very old man. Spite? Vengeance? Intimidation? Simple meanness?"

"I think they must have gotten wind of your aggressive timeline and were trying to slow you all down. Probably a competitor who is not quite ready to go to market yet and worried about losing control if you get there first. I'm guessing our informer shared everything with them and they reacted preemptively. I'm worried about what they might try next."

"Nothing is going to stop us, William. Nothing."

Reports at the Monday staff meeting bore out Dr. Randall's resolve.

Robert announced that Assistant Professor Means had disappeared in totality, even from his teaching obligations at the university. No one knew where he had gone. "There is no doubt that he was the leaker and had fed everything we shared, including the business plan, to someone, probably a competitor, on a regular basis. His betrayal had led to the assassination attempt on Dr. Randall and attempt to engage, or worse, Heni and Henry in the hotel. All with the intent of slowing us down or driving us away from our efforts to bring product to market."

Who or whatever was behind the violence was obviously a threat to all of them. That said, the finish line loomed ahead and the push toward it demanded full commitment. If anything strange or threatening surfaces, Robert asked all to report it to him immediately.

Otherwise, extreme vigilance must be the rule of the day and night.

Again, any who wanted out was welcome to leave. No one did.

Professor Madison and Henry Hoary confirmed that a long-term lease had been signed on an old, nondescript warehouse located on a remote farm just outside of town. Its heavily wooded surroundings provided cover and seclusion. Two large stainless steel tanks were due for delivery at the end of the week, and one should be boiling creek water delivered by tanker in the middle of the night shortly thereafter. They would not ramp up production to three tankers per day until a primitive bottling line could be installed, tested, and operated on an efficient basis. The initial production runs should be fully functioning two weeks out, right in line with Dr. Randall's original schedule.

Dr. Thrush reported on his meeting with Dr. Randall, noting that he was pretty down about his prognosis. He would likely not walk again and would wear a colostomy bag going forward. He was frank to admit that the only thing making it worth living was the work all of you are doing to bring the product to millions in need. He is strong in his support of your commitment but will not be rejoining us for some time. He is really not in any condition to see any of us at this time, either.

Thrush also confirmed the continuation of extremely high cure and prevention rates in his unit and his confidence as a scientist and outsider that the Clear Creek Elixir worked as promised. He would continue his testing protocols until ready to go public.

Henry had rented multiple storefronts in St. Louis and Springfield and had begun to hire college students to provide twenty-four-hour staffing in case demand took off as hoped. Means was to have looked at expanding distribution points regionally and nationally, but that would simply have to wait for now. "Good riddance," Henry had added.

All eyes were on Professor Barnes, Rachel, and Robert as they laid out their marketing and promotional strategy. Rachel had completed a draft of the blockbuster magazine issue that Heni had begun, Robert had begun to reach out to various news agencies in anticipation of providing an earthshaking press release about the coronavirus, and Lori was in the midst of providing a longer-term marketing strategy to reach millions over time. In two weeks, the world would know all about Clear Creek Elixir.

Lauren McCall had drafted final easement and estate documents for the property owners to execute, which would assure product supply far into the future.

Henry was able to confirm that Heni and Emma Marie were thriving, and there was even talk of setting a date for their return home. Henry would, of course, go with them and depend on Robert to provide backup administration for distribution points. Henry hoped to be leaving with Heni within the week. While he was excited about the product rollout, it was nothing compared to holding his new daughter.

"We're only saving the world," goaded Professor Madison.

"For my Emma Marie," Henry responded, blinking back tears.

The Clear Creek Elixir Express was chugging ahead on all cylinders.

chapter thirty-nine

SNATCHED

"WE'VE GOT HIM," THE HEAVILY ACCENTED VOICE WHISPERED INTO THE PHONE. "The little bastard is ours, and his colleagues have but forty-eight hours to provide us with product and source. A message to that effect has been delivered to one Robert Winchell, who is purportedly the lead dog for the operation."

Henry had returned home with Heni and the baby as planned, leaving the project and his colleagues behind. He didn't notice the tailers who observed his every movement.

It took them only forty-eight hours to nab him as he returned to his car from the grocery store, gun in his back, gag in his mouth. They took him to a deserted office building in a small town, ironically bearing the name and within walking distance of the very creek they were looking for. The building had been owned for years by an immigrant from Petralux who had remained a loyalist and in contact with his native government. His reasons for settling in such a remote location related to a woman from there, who had worked in the US Embassy in his home country. He had pursued her romantically several years back, including visiting her hometown with her on several occasions. He had fallen out of love with her but in love with the place. It was a long and strange story.

Henry was kept blindfolded and bound in a darkened room up a flight of stairs and provided only with water on occasion. He had no contact with any of his abductors and didn't even know how many there were. He could barely hear a TV playing somewhere, probably downstairs. He had no idea why or where but knew that he had to try and escape.

When Heni was advised of the ransom note by Robert, she was already desperate and had brought in local law officials to look for Henry. The reason for his disappearance only heightened her despair, and the threat to kill him was met with panic and disbelief. She could only beg Robert to meet the terms of the kidnappers and bring Henry home to his family.

Robert met with Rachel to discuss their options. They could do nothing and try to call the abductors bluff, if indeed it was that. Or they could accede to their demands, provide a bottle of the elixir and a map to Crane Creek, and hope that Henry would be released or returned. There really wasn't much in between to consider.

Rachel pointed out that releasing the product and source could eventually get it to market. Even if not free or widely distributed, it would save lives. That might be worth Henry's life?

Releasing source information would violate their sacred vow to the Campbells to protect their precious creek from exploitation or worse, noted Robert, with no assurance that Henry would be returned.

There was no certainty with any course of action, and they were running out of time.

Henry was finally able to untie the knot that secured his hands, utilizing his teeth. He crossed to a small curtained window, which revealed dull light outside. He had to step carefully to avoid his own puddles of urine and a pile of feces, as they had made him void himself on the floor under their watchful eye. He heard steps mounting the staircase and quickly rewrapped the rope around his wrists.

An accented voice warned that his forty-eight hours was almost up, whatever that meant. That this would be his last water unless their ransom request was honored. The door slammed shut after his captor. He wondered what they had asked for.But not for long. This was it, Henry figured. He had to make a break or something bad was going to happen. He was able to wedge through the small window and grab a drain downspout to slide hesitantly down. With his feet on solid ground, he surveyed his surroundings.

The first thing that greeted his squinting eyes was a giant billboard announcing:

"THE 68th ANNUAL CRANE BROILER FESTIVAL—2020"

Beneath the headline was a photo of a buxom young lady wearing a crown with the headline of "Miss Slick Chick, 2019."

He looked beyond the billboard and noticed a casket business next door. It appeared to be open. The sign said BLUE SHIELD CASKET COMPANY, Crane, Missouri. He panicked when he saw Crane Creek meandering in the distance. Maybe that was what this was all about?

He slipped along the side of his former place of incarceration, then dashed for the adjacent front door. A handsome young man greeted him with a smile.

"I need help, sir. My name is Henry Hoary from Springfield, and I have been held captive next door for I don't know how long. Hours? Days? I know there is a ransom involved, and I've got to get hold of my wife."

"My name is Jaime, and if you want to avoid the ones next door, you had better jump into this demo casket right now." He pointed at the three men moving quickly from the office building he had been in.

"Thank you, Jaime," he muttered as he jumped into the empty casket that Jaime had opened up for him.

"Good afternoon, gentlemen. How can I assist you?"

"Have you seen a young man wandering around outside? Tall, dark-haired, in his twenties or thirties?" The heavy accent threw Jaime. It was like that of the guy who owned the building next door.

"No, it's been a quiet afternoon. I have seen no one."

"You had better be leveling with us or you might find yourself in one of these," a second man warned, kicking the casket Henry lay quietly in.

"I tell you nothing but the truth, sir."

"Fair enough. We will be watching you. If you see a stranger, better to alert us immediately," he ordered, slamming the door behind him.

"Yes, sir."

Jaime waited a couple of minutes before opening the casket to free an ashen-faced Henry.

"Is this what it is like to die? Jammed into a box without light or air, strange voices all around, without one of your own? I think I want to be cremated. Do you know those goons, Jaime?"

Jaime laughed before answering, "No, but the owner of the building is from a small Eastern European country with a crazy name. He speaks with the same distinct accent. I can tell they are no good. The question becomes "How can we get you out of here without them knowing?". They have posted at least two positions, one in front and the other behind the building."

"I don't know, but I've got to call my wife immediately."

"Well, our cell service in spotty, but I can drive you up to the top of the hill above the creek and try. My landline is down temporarily, or we could use that. We don't really need much phone service to do what I do around here."

"Whatever you say."

"I say get back in the casket, and I'll roll you out to my old hearse in the back."

"I have to get back in there again? It's awful."

"Well, it's the safest option, I think. They will probably stop me and search the vehicle if I take you in my car. If I tell them I'm delivering a cadaver to Springfield, I doubt they will want to dig too deep. I'll drive you on up there once you have made your phone call."

Henry hesitated, then nodded.

"Better let me wrap you in this burial gown in case they insist on taking a look. My grandmother made it."

Henry grimaced, wrapped up, and climbed back in the casket as Jaime shut the lid on him once again. Jaime' rolled the casket out to his hearse, pushed it into the back, and stopped by the lookout on his way out.

"Taking a body to Springfield. Be back in a couple of hours."

"It's a real dead body?" he asked with trepidation.

"Yes."

"Get it out of here."

"Good luck with your search," Jaime shouted as he waved goodbye.

Jaime freed Henry from the confines of the casket once they were clear of town and headed up the hill in search of cell phone reception.

"Heni, it's me. I'm safe."

Silence. Then sobs and "Oh, Henry. I'm so thankful."

"Reception is poor where I am, and I'll call back once we are closer to town."

"What is 'we' and 'where'?"

"Will tell you everything shortly."

Heni called Robert immediately to let him know that she had heard from Henry. "I don't know anything," Heni repeated over and over as Robert peppered her with questions. "I only know that he is safe."

"You've saved my life, Jaime. I can never repay you."

"No need to, Henry. Good deeds are hard to stumble onto these days, and I'm grateful to have a chance to do one.

"Do you know the Campbells, Jaime? Esther and Hobart?"

"Yep. They live out on the creek. I was very worried about them earlier in the year. Esther got very sick, and we all feared that it was corona. And then all of a sudden she was well and healthier than ever. None of us could ever figure that one out."

"Just wait, Jaime, just wait."

"You know them and about them?"

"Yes. I used to access the creek for trout through their property. It was the virus, and I know how she licked it. You won't believe it!"

"Wow, can't wait for this one."

"So, what country are you from, Jaime'?"

"Pure born, full-blooded Republican American, just like my daddy and his before him."

"But the name? Jaime? Jaime what?"

"Jaime Insecta Smith. Don't have a clue where it came from. Maybe one of my parents' old boy- or girlfriends? Maybe an inside joke between them? Who knows?"

"Catchy. . . ."

"He got away, comrade, he has escaped. Our deal is dead."

chapter forty

THE FINISH LINE

"**W**E'VE DONE IT, TEAM. TOMORROW, PROFESSOR MADISON DOES HIS INAUGURAL run of Clear Creek Elixir. Henry will begin stocking his storefronts. Two days later, Rachel's press release announcing the release of Heni's blockbuster edition of *Midwestern Viewpoint Magazine*, detailing a cure and prevention of the coronavirus, goes viral. In just four days, Clear Creek Elixir will be available to the world. The press release is complete, with one exception, and the magazine is at the printer. All of this accomplished in just over thirty days, despite critical and life-threatening obstacles, because of you."

"I suggest that the first copy of the first run be delivered to Dr. Irving Randall in his hospital bed," shouted Henry, hanging on tightly to Heni.

"Amen," seconded Rachel, to applause and shouts around the room.

Robert had one more order of business to complete. "I need a few photographs to accompany the press release. Rachel's assistant will handle." He passed out small bottles of the elixir to everyone and raised his in a toast. "We can finally shed our veil of secrecy and celebrate with the world. Here's to Clear Creek kicking the coronavirus's ass." He chugged his down, as did the others. "We won't need our masks anymore," he crowed, tossing his into the air, again followed by the others.

The photographer captured the toast, the chug-a-lug, the rain of masks, and the beaming faces to soon share with the public.

"Our press release is ready to go, sir."

"Will it come out the logo of Pharma-Lax, Inc., or a pseudonym?"

"That of course will be up to you, sir. Our strong preference is that it come directly from us, a selfless act of goodwill, seeking to protect people around the world from a scam. Hiding behind a fictitious front would surely be exposed at some point, particularly given the amount of money we will be spending, and might turn the public against us. Why not be up front about our genuine and well-founded concerns and stand up like the experts in infectious diseases we are? We're the good guys in this battle, the ones with a real vaccine that is being properly tested under strict regulatory eye, not a ragtag group of random pretenders peddling bottled water with here-to-now unknown side effects. We might even get a couple of our corporate colleagues to join us for the sake of credibility and a small piece of the action."

"Makes perfect sense, Deputy Smith. Tell me more about the release."

"It demonizes Dr. Irving Randall as a soulless fraud, documents his previous attempts to doctor important test results, and accompanies a letter to the editor of every major newspaper in the United States, signed by over fifty respected giants of science, demeaning Randall's credibility and professional record. It begs people not to fall victim to a hoax and warns of risks to health and well-being for anyone who samples Clear Creek Elixir because of the lack of a proper testing protocol and US government clearance and certification. More importantly, it promises a safe and cheap vaccine, thoroughly vetted and tested by proper authorities, within five months."

"Excellent. When will it post?"

"The very day they send their press release out, which will likely be lightweight and focus attention on the subsequent article in their magazine. At least that is how their business plan reads."

"But we can't stop there, Deputy Smith."

"We won't. We will seek to discredit *Midwestern Viewpoint Magazine* as a partisan liberal rag, including damaging quotes from previous articles. Then a more detailed exposé of Dr. Irving Randall's many sins. At least three installments of that, rotating around character assassination pieces on each respective team member. And even a blurry Photoshopped image of leader Robert Winchell with a naked, self-identified hooker who will speak of his grandiose self-expressions of greatness and desire to get very rich from his new product promotion. All of this over the next two weeks."

"That's better."

"Not finished yet, sir. We will parade a series of scientific experts onto radio talk and call-in shows to decry Randall and his whole process of rushed product development. Social media will be abuzz with rumors of serious illness or even death from ingesting the elixir, and we have paid a half dozen 'victims' a lot of money to go on camera and speak to the terrible side effects they have experienced after just one sip of the poison."

"And this will buy us the time to finish properly testing our vaccine, receive FDA approval, CDC and WHO recommendations, close on lucrative deals with other nations to buy product as we roll it out, in most cases distributing it free of charge to the masses, making it price competitive with Clear Creek Elixir, ridding the world of this dreadful pandemic and making multimillionaires of us all? How is that for a mouthful?"

"Yes, sir, Mr. CEO. Yes, sir! We are performing a public service in the interest of humanity."

"Well done, Smith. Spare no expense or mistruth in your efforts."

Dr. Thrush and Rachel Roberts, as the only team members cleared to visit Dr. Randall, still in intensive care, delivered copy number one to his bedside personally.

Thrush spoke first. "The team sends their love and respect, Irving, and wants you to have the first copy from the first run of Heni's magazine feature. Each has signed and included a personal message. The press release announcing the special edition of *Midwestern Viewpoint Magazine* goes out tomorrow. It will be an exciting day for the world and a proud day for you. This could not have happened without you, Irving."

Dr. Randall could only nod and smile weakly.

Rachel added that all were anxious to see him, but she was keeping him under lock and key for the time being in the interest of his health. The interview Heni had conducted with him prior to his disablement would be the story lead-in. Heni and Ethel Campbell (anonymous) would also provide lengthy personal testimony. Rachel assured him it was a most powerful piece. This evoked only a glazed look from him.

Thrush glanced at Rachel briefly, and both excused themselves.

"He looks terrible, Rachel, almost a hopelessness in his eyes. And this at his moment of supreme accomplishment. It's just not like him."

"You are correct, William. He is deeply depressed. We have tried any number of antis on him, to no avail. It's like he's lost his will to live."

"Just as he has brought life to so many."

"Sad. Very sad."

chapter forty-one

THE AFTERMATH

"WHAT? THIS CAN'T BE!" SHOUTED ROBERT, LEAPING FROM RACHEL'S BED.

He had been scrolling down his news feed, waiting for her to awaken to share reporting on her press release. Instead he found a massive condemnation of Dr. Randall, Clear Creek Elixir, and their whole project. "Who the hell is Pharma-Lax, Inc?"

"What is it, Robert?"

"Who is Pharma-Lax, Inc?"

"They are a mega multinational drug conglomerate who purportedly are closing in on a government-approved corona vaccine."

"I thought I had heard of them. My God, they are the ones who have been trying to sabotage us, who shot Irving, who kidnapped Henry, who paid Means for our business plan. It has to have been them. Read this."

"Where's my release?"

"You have been preempted, my love."

And so it was that the world came to know about the cure of and protection from the coronavirus promised by Clear Creek Elixir.

The subsequent release of Heni's breathtaking issue of *Midwestern Viewpoint Magazine* was completely overshadowed by the massive Pharma-Lax campaign to discredit everyone and everything related to the elixir.

A few curious souls wandered into Henry's storefronts. But there was no rush to be saved. Only fear. It didn't matter that the product was available and free. It was too tainted with doubt and corruption to be trusted. There were even a couple of really sick elderly people who drank it down and claimed to be cured. Laughable to most.

The Pharma-Lax strategy worked. Corporate colleagues stood up behind Pharma-Lax's claims. Even the US government spoke against lack of testing protocols for Clear Creek Elixir and their inability to endorse a product that had not been properly vetted.

A growing number of foreign governments, including Petralux, lined up to order Pharma-Lax in five months. Not Clear Creek, immediately. All planned to deliver the Pharma-Lax product quickly and for free when it became available. All paid heavily for the privilege of doing so.

Robert and his comrades were stunned. None had seen this coming. The Pharma-Lax campaign discredited them to perfection, and all his team could do was try to counter their arguments and offer the elixir to any who would try it. Without a corresponding bankroll to share success stories or ridicule ridiculous rumors, an international and national marketing plan turned local and regional with only limited success.

They considered legal action, but attorney Lauren McCall counseled against it because of potential cost and lack of solid evidence of malfeasance.

The Pharma-Lax product, Effisal, was delivered a month late, but with great fanfare. Vaccine test results were trumpeted around the world, confirmed by the FDA, and recommended by the WHO. The pandemic was stopped in its tracks. People were protected once sovereign distribution caught up with supply, demand, and favoritism. Kickbacks were encouraged, the rich and powerful went first, and fortunes were made.

They even discovered the partially charred remains of Associate Professor Leonard Means in a small, heavily wooded state park along the Mississippi River. A couple of teen campers stumbled on the gruesome evidence, and a DNA match confirmed his fate. No one or entity was ever charged, although it was a clearly case of homicide.

In the interim between Pharma-Lax's initial attack and product delivery, a half million more people around the globe died, and ten times that many were newly infected. A heavy price to pay for corporate deception and greed.

chapter forty-two

TRANSITIONS

ROBERT TRIED TO KEEP HIS TEAM OF VIRUS WARRIORS TOGETHER, BUT INTEREST AND energy was clearly waning in the wake of Pharma-Lax's surge to the front of coronavirus prevention.

Though Dr. Thrush had to return to his home base, Rachel continued to direct her physicians to treat corona-infected patients with Clear Creek Elixir with the resultant same success rate. Her public pronouncements of effective treatment were not accorded the attention garnered daily by Pharma-Lax's mighty PR machine and were frequently discredited by the same. Adding Thrush's imminence and endorsement of the elixir could not offset the damage to Dr. Randall's credibility inflicted by the constant Pharma-Lax attacks and revisitations of his discrediting decades earlier.

And when they turned the spotlight on Rachel's past promiscuity and current cohabitation with Clear Creek Elixir's project leader, she threw up her hands and bunkered down with Robert.

Ethel Campbell died. But not of the coronavirus. She suffered a massive brain aneurysm out of the blue, which took her quickly.

Hobart buried her atop the hill overlooking Crane Creek but not before dipping her in the ice-cold waters in hopes of just one more miracle. The small burial service was poignant and emotional.

He told Henry and Heni afterwards that he couldn't bear to stay in his cabin alone and would be moving into an assisted living facility in Springfield. As promised, the fully furnished cabin, including land and memories, would be turned over to them as soon as he was relocated, and he would sign whatever paperwork was required to expedite the legal process. He wanted it to be theirs as a final act of love for Ethel.

Professor James Madison headed back to the classroom, shaking his head in disbelief and leaving Henry in charge of his abbreviated production line. Henry continued to pump out product but at a vastly reduced level to avoid overloading shelf space in his now down to two storefronts. Professor Barnes had nothing more to add and followed Madison back to school. Attorney Lauren McCall stayed involved on specific legal matters, such as transitioning ownership of the Crane Creek property to Heni and Henry, but only as a favor to her friend Robert.

One of Pharma-Lax's most brutal attacks was a personal one on Heni. Calling her a "Black prostitute" who once stabbed a man to death when he wouldn't pay her for three days of sexual favors, they challenged the Springfield sheriff's office to reopen their investigation into the murder of one Ed Jones. They ran interviews with two sheriff deputies who questioned why Henrietta White had been let off so quickly and without consequences after their multiple interrogations had disclosed a lot of empty holes in her testimony. She had claimed there was no sex involved, but no authority had even swabbed her to check for DNA tracks. They wondered if she had ridden the "white coattails" of her "squeeze of the moment" and supported the notion of further investigation.

This was the final indignity in a mountain of same to be showered upon the coronavirus warriors and lovers.

chapter forty-three

REFLECTIONS

SHELL-SHOCKED HENI AND HENRY SOON RETREATED TO THEIR NEW HILLTOP PARADISE, high above Crane Creek, with baby Ella, still trying to figure out exactly what had hit them.

"How could we have prevented this failure to save lives?" Heni asked one evening.

"Perhaps we did, Heni. The virus is under control, the spreading has stopped, life around the world is returning to some semblance of normalcy. Maybe we had something to do with that. Maybe we never had any business even trying to compete with an international juggernaut, which had massive distribution and information dissemination systems already ensconced in the global fabric. But maybe our presence hastened their progress in producing a vaccine, if not a cure.

"Could we have saved more lives if we had come out earlier? Yes. But without government sanctioning amidst a general skepticism about vaccines in general and our lack of public profile, who knows if we could have sold the public, expanded our reach, and prevented more corona deaths than the bastards at Pharma-Lax in the end? It doesn't much matter now, does it?"

"What do you think about the accusations that your 'white privilege' somehow got me out of a murder charge."

"I don't even know what 'white privilege' means, Heni. Sure, I'm white as a sheet, but did that earn me you? Is 'white privilege' having a Black true love and an amazing tan daughter?"

"Of course not. But perhaps it provided you with advantages growing up, access to education and employment, think about it. You claim to have had no Black girlfriends?"

"Not before you."

"Did you even have any Black friends? Did anyone of color ever offer an opportunity to you, open a door for you, assure that you had a chance to compete?"

"Not really. I grew up in the Mozarks, hon."

"Did you ever interact with Blacks in higher positions than you? Before Robert? Did you ever work with a Black man of equal position or level of compensation? Did you ever open a door to opportunity for anyone of color?"

"No. Look, why are we even talking about this? You are confusing me, Heni."

"It's not a simple subject, Henry. My guess is that a white male helped you get everything you've gotten in life. A solid footing to start with. An education. A job."

"Stop it, Heni. You are really starting to piss me off."

"Good. Because it really pissed me off that those white sheriff's deputies could accuse me of ducking a thorough murder investigation and possible conviction because of my white boyfriend. Not because I was innocent but because you were there to call off the dogs and open the door for me to escape through."

"You got off because you are innocent, not because of anyone's color."

"I'm not so sure, Henry, not so sure."

"I don't want to talk about it, this 'white privilege' bullshit."

"Most white males don't, Henry, and that's the problem. White privilege exists, at the expense of equal opportunity, intended or not, for most people of color. And women for that matter. And until this reality is faced, discussed, and understood, it will never be confronted or changed. You are a wonderful man, Henry, and I love you as I have never loved before. You have fathered my daughter, with others to come I hope. You have lifted me up, helped me become more, and I will always be grateful. But you are the product of a white privileged upbringing and society. And if it weren't for you, I could possibly be festering in some jail cell for killing a poor white Sunday School teaching martyr-pervert because he purportedly wouldn't pay for my sexual favors."

"So, are you now saying that you are grateful for my 'white privilege'?"

"No. I'm saying that I am grateful for you, grateful to lie next to you every night, white or not. And that I possibly wouldn't have that privilege if you were not white."

"What do you want me to say, Heni?"

"Just that you won't forget this conversation with me and agree to continue it into our future. It's important to me. It's important to little Emma. And it is important to the society and country in which we live."

And often of an early afternoon, after putting Emma down for a nap, Heni would stroll down the hill behind their cabin, remove her clothing piece by piece, and lie down in the healing waters of Crane Creek. Henry would watch in wonder, marveling at her beauty and deep shade of ebony, sometimes thinking back to the first time he saw her sultry striptease.

So much had happened since that late spring afternoon two years earlier. True love, a baby, a farmhouse, a global pandemic, a cure, a vaccine, a stabbing in self-defense, a kidnapping, character assassinations, shootings, murders, and on and on and on. All in the context of a magical creek. It was almost too much to comprehend. And, yet, he wouldn't trade one piece of it if the remainder was compromised or lost.

Often, Henry would wander down after watching awhile, and join Heni in the water, flesh tingling at the chill. When he thought to take a blanket to spread out on the grass, they would make love. He called it "coronalove."

"In the end isn't that what we are left with, Heni? 'Coronalove.' A love that can't be broken."

chapter forty-four

TIRED

D R. IRVING RANDALL WAS TIRED. NO ONE WAS MORE DESPONDENT OVER THE Pharma-Lax, Inc., power play and resultant unnecessary loss of life.

His active physical life had been reduced by a single bullet to being permanently bedridden.. His mental and emotional health soon followed. It wasn't just the blanket of mistruths spread about him, the discrediting of his character and motivations. It was the failure of humanity to once again stand up to corporate bullying, to bow to monied interests, to lick the boot of the self-serving oppressor. It was the failure of most everyone to recognize the superiority of Clear Creek Elixir as both therapy and immunity booster, lost in a public relations blitz of promotional mistruths and downright lies. It was the half million additional souls who didn't need to die.

Disillusioned, hurt, and depressed, Irving Randall asked his old friend William Thrush to come back for a visit.

"Bill, I need your help."

"Whatever I can do, Irving."

"I can't bear to live anymore. I can't walk. I can only shit in a bag. I piss myself constantly and hate diaper rash. I have bedsores and deep bruises all over from brushing up against anything. And that's only the physical part. It's my mind that hurts more."

Dr. Thrush looked deep into his eyes and saw only hopelessness.

"We presented the world with a natural solution to a devastating virus, from prevention to cure. A truly altruistic undertaking to better humanity, not make a few people rich, very rich. And we were rejected, maligned, and exiled. I can't stand it anymore, Bill. I need to die."

"What are you asking me, Irving?"

"Kill me, Bill."

"You want me to help you leave this world behind? Are you talking doctor-assisted suicide? Or do you just want me to get you a gun? Or push you out an open window? To do any of the above in this place and time could get me imprisoned for the rest of my life. Accomplice to a murder. Think about what you are asking."

"I know what I'm asking. Sorry. It's not for you to kill me. It is for you to provide me with the means to kill myself. Get me some secobarbital, Bill. I can do the rest."

"I can't do it in Missouri, Irving. Only eight states and the District of Columbia would allow me to help you die. Colorado is the closest one, and you are in no shape to make that journey, take up residency, and wait out the eligibility requirements."

"Can't you just slip a bottle of the 'reds,' I think they call them, under my pillow?"

"No, that would be violating my oath as a doctor to heal, not harm.

"And there is a larger issue here. Do you have a right to take your own life no matter how miserable?"

"Why not?"

"You've had more than your share of ups and downs through your eight decades, Irving. More incredible high points than deep valleys, I would venture. You are in a deep trough now and may be for the rest of your days. Isn't that the price all of us pay someday? If we are lucky enough to live as long as you have in relatively good health?"

"I want to die, Bill. If you won't help me, I'll find another way."

"I'm sorry, Irving. You know what high regard I have always held you in. I'm disillusioned too. The bad guys won. The good guys lost. And at least a half million people died that shouldn't have. I'm sorry that you feel compelled to add your name to that list."

A week later Dr. Irving Randall rolled over on his side and stuffed his hand under his pillow for balance. He encountered an object. It was a bottle of pills. He pulled them forth to examine and smiled at what he saw. An unmarked bottle filled with red capsules.

Twenty-four hours later, Dr. Irving Randall was dead. With a smile on his face for the first time in months. No one asked. No one told.

His life was celebrated at a reception hosted by Rachel Roberts at the hospital. He had died under her care and mysterious circumstances, and she owed him that.

A few of his ashes were sprinkled in Crane Creek and spread on the ground around his cabin in Protem.

chapter forty-five

HITCHED

"HENI, WILL YOU FINALLY MARRY ME? I HAVE BEEN ASKING YOU FOR MONTHS, AND you always seem to slip the question. We are best of friends and lovers, mother and father, partners and patrons. Please marry me now, Heni, please."

"We have talked about this for a while, haven't we? Well, why not? I don't need it, but obviously you do. No ritual, no pledging of our love, no public spectacle will bring us closer together. Or keep us there.

"No 'till death do us part' will guaranty that. Only we can do that as we grow up and into each other. It's actually pretty male and whitish of you to ask, Henry!"

"No more white male privilege bullshit just now, Heni!"

"Nope. And, yes, I will marry you, Henry."

Six months after their retreat to Ethel and Hobart's farm from a world healing of corona, if not greed, Heni and Henry were wed atop the hill behind the house, facing down to beautiful Crane Creek.

Heni wore a simple white dress, her ebony skin a striking contrast to the bright white. Not to bow to tradition but to honor her maiden name she announced proudly mid-ceremony. Henrietta White Hoary. She cradled little Emma Marie in her arms as she spoke of her love for Henry and her baby. She made no vows, explaining that vows were made to be broken. Coronalove could not—be broken, that is.

Henry broke down and tied a tie around his neck. He also broke down and cried at the mention of coronalove. He promised to love Heni and Emma forever and beyond, earning a smile from his mate.

Witnesses included Hobart, who sat in a wheelchair, gazing out at his creek, thinking of Ethel; Robert and Rachel, arms interlocked; and every other living member of the Clear Creek Elixir team, gathered together for the first time in months. Lauren McCall presided, lending legal legitimacy to the proceedings. Lori Barnes offered a short blessing covering the religious bases. There were no "I dos" or "I won'ts", "I takes" or "I gives" per Heni's request. Henry did grab the bride and lay a big one on her as the service transitioned informally to celebration. Champagne was served in paper cups. Smoked McCloud trout and fried Crane Creek frog legs were spread out on a picnic table, along with a large bowl of dilled potato salad Heni had prepared using Ethel's favorite old recipe. Only she and Dr. Irving Randall were missing, both toasted multiple times.

The sun shone bright on the small band of corona warriors, and the creek that had brought them together, as coronalove coalesced around them.

Heni and Henry still had to pinch themselves occasionally. Ethel and Hobart's farm was theirs now, title vested in their names only, transferred for the price of $1.00. They had become as children to the elderly couple and were treated accordingly.

Henry had quit his job at MSU during the race to bring Clear Creek Elixir to the finish line and devoted his full efforts to setting up retail outlets and later running the bottling line, though at much reduced capacity. He was paid a living wage out of Dr. Randall's bankroll, which continued after the former's passing. He would never be rich but plugged away at getting bottles of the elixir on shelves in the storefronts he still maintained in Springfield and St. Louis. He was able to continue to give away a few of the small bottles as a coronavirus cure and immunity booster, but the virus was under control, and the fortunes had been banked. He sometimes wondered what life would be like if they had been first to market without a competing product or massive PR campaign sabotage, how many millions of lives they would have saved with their magic creek water? But not for long. Beyond the bitter and deep wounds to Dr. Randall and Heni, he could not have dreamed a better outcome.

Crane Creek ran as clear and pure as it always had. No one or entity had ever been able to finger it as source of the elixir, and as such, it was protected from notoriety and exploitation.

It was so ironic to Henry that he had been held hostage less than 100 yards away from the prize his kidnappers had desired to trade him for. He never did determine if they were sponsored by Pharma-Lax, Inc., or a strange but real competing Eastern European offshoot. He would always be grateful to Jaime Insecta Smith for saving his life, and they became close family friends with him and his family. Jaime, his wife Diana, and their three young children would often come to picnic in Henry and Heni's backyard, and splash around in pristine Crane Creek. Emma got to join in as she grew and developed. She particularly loved the icy cold water and would squeak with delight when Heni dipped her under.

Emma also loved the chickens and the cow that Henry had added to the mix that first summer. She would waddle after the chickens in their free-range enclosure and learned to eat the funny-looking eggs they produced.

A gentleman farmer Henry liked to dub himself, which meant that he left the cow milking to Heni. She actually enjoyed it and the peace it brought to her.

With no further investigation into her stabbing and killing of Ed Jones in self-defense, despite the initiative Pharma-Lax, Inc., sponsored to reopen the case, the trauma and hurt slipped to the back of her mind. Pulling on udders and producing healthy milk for the family to drink kept it there. It seemed like so long ago, just like the rest of her life before Henry, though it was in fact less than a few years past.

Henry was anxious to introduce little Emma to a float trip but bowed to Heni's request to wait one more summer.

"She's so developed for a near yearling," Henry had argued. "Look at her run around. She can even stay afloat in the creek by splashing arms and legs together. I think her rate of development is almost supernatural. This girl is going to be something special."

Not that Heni disagreed, but her one and only float trip memory featuring the racist rants of ol' Redneck Rectum was a caution flag.

And that particular creek was the only one with adequate water at this point. Sadly, Crane Creek would probably never be floatable. Only walkable, which was good enough for her.

"That was a long time back, hon."

"Not really."

chapter forty-six

A FLOAT TRIP

I T WAS LATE SUMMER WHEN THEY FINALLY LOADED NEARLY TWO-YEAR-OLD EMMA IN Henry's old gray canoe, sitting in her own little chair between Heni's legs in the bow. The sun was out, but storms were in the forecast. Henry hoped to get them in well before anything broke. No night out tonight.

He remembered well doing the same to Heni three years earlier, same time, same place, and the nightmare that had followed. Though this was his favorite floating stream, he had wanted another but had found them lacking in water. So, here they were, but no nightmares today. Emma was in for a treat.

The preceding year had flown by. Little Emma continued her rapid rate of development. Precocious and coordinated, she was the life of their lives. They snuggled around winter fires for heat and love.

They took turns reading aloud to Emma every night. Both remembered the same from their youth. Heni's mother, exhausted but lifted by her daughter's enthusiastic embrace of the stories, had rarely missed a night. Heni never ceased the joy of listening and learning new words. Henry got it from both mom and dad, alone or together, and was soon talking wildly and widely.

Emma surpassed them both as best they could recall. When she dropped a couple of double syllable words on them, recall became fact.

"Child prodigy?" Heni wondered aloud one cold evening.

"Not from my blood line," Henry wondered back.

And, somehow, Emma was going to have a friend. Heni was PG, not planned but not denied, baby due winter 2023.

Spring and summer had brought a surge in outdoor activities.

It was Emma's innate love of all things natural and outdoors, even at such an early stage, that amazed them most. At less than two years old, she was turning over rocks in Crane Creek and pulling out crawdads, even holding them behind the ears to avoid pinchers.

And then there was the baby copperhead she presented proudly, wrapped lightly around her wrist. Henry knew what it was but also not to risk grabbing it and prompting a strike. Besides the eight-or-so-inch light brown poisonous snake with the yellow tail had seemed strangely calm in Emma's grasp.

"Need to put snake down, Em."

Emma smiled back and shook her head. "Please, Emma, put the snake on the ground and let it crawl away. It might die if you keep holding it."

This thought made Emma frown and walk back to the woodpile where she had found it, slowly bend down, and allow it to unwind and crawl away.

"Don't move, hon, you might scare it."

Emma stood stone-still as it crawled back under the woodpile, then waved her small hand "Goodbye, copperhead," she said. Henry could only shake his head in wonder.

He would have to remember to come back and check for others, as well as relocate this one across the creek. He wasn't sure he should even tell Heni. About the snake . . . or the word.

And now a float trip.

Henry shoved them into the current, Emma squealing at the wonder of it all. She kept reaching over the side to touch the water rushing by and being pulled back into her seat by Mom. They finally just tossed her overboard, little life jacket securely attached to a bow rope, dangling in Heni's grasp.

Henry caught a fish or two, which warranted a lift back in the canoe, so Emma could kiss them goodbye before Henry's release. Otherwise, they couldn't get her out of the water, even for lunch, which she ate sitting in the shallows.

Midafternoon Henry noticed a gathering of thunderheads on the horizon, moving quickly toward them. The forecast storms were arriving ahead of schedule, and he picked up the paddling pace to try and beat them to take-out.

Not to be. A couple of lightning bolts and pelting rain turned their rapture into discomfort and concern. As Henry paddled around a bend, he noticed a tarp shelter securely attached to several trees on a far gravel bar. Not thinking, he pulled toward it, before realizing that this was the very gravel bar he and Heni had been run off with a vicious racist rant their first float together. He pulled in, nonetheless, wanting to get his ladies out of the downpour.

They sat under cover, huddled together for warmth, with nary a whimper from Emma, who seemed almost amused by the thunder and lightning around them. Suddenly, the sound of a four-wheeler was upon them, loosing a torrent of nasty memories in both Heni and Henry. Heni pulled Emma even closer to her body.

This time it was a young man about their age who pulled up.

"I seen you all paddling in and hoped you would take cover under my tarp. I leave it here just for occasions like this, as well as to camp under with my two boys. Are you all OK? Name is Fern, Fern Foster. And you all go by?"

"I'm Henry, this is Heni, and little Emma on her first float trip."

"Picked a dandy day to go, huh?"

"It was beautiful until an hour ago. OK if we huddle here until the worst is over?"

"No, Henry, that is precisely the reason I came racing down here. There is worse weather heading in, tornado warnings and the like, and the creek will soon be on a rapid rise. I would like to take you all back to my house to ride it out, spend the night, and let the creek settle down."

"Oh, we don't want to impose," pleaded Heni, turning over the image of a fat, overalled redneck threatening to kill them in the back of her mind.

"It is no imposition, ma'am, in fact I insist."

"Thank you, Fern. It's just that we had a very unpleasant experience on this property several years ago, related to my wife's race, and—"

Fern chuckled. "It wasn't just you. And racism was just one of his major flaws. My dear deceased father was an asshole, plain and simple. He forgot to raise me to be one. Come on now, folks, let's get settled in before it gets worse."

"Thank you, Fern."

One wrong righted, another memorable float trip on the books, and Emma hooked for life.

chapter forty-seven

PIGS AND PERMITS

"**H**OW MANY ACRES DO YOU HAVE HERE, SON?"

The knock on the door had been loud and persistent, and the knocker presented as an overweight, self-identified businessman.

"A hundred or so, I guess. Why?"

"I don't suppose you would be interested in parting with it for a price well above the current market? I am representing a buyer from out of state who is seeking a large tract of stream front property to retire on. He has already acquired a sizable parcel along Crane Creek just upstream from you."

"Do you mean the Adams' spread? I know they are elderly and in poor health with heirs spread all around the country, but I thought they would at least talk to me first."

"You never would have offered them what my client did, son. Would you believe 50 percent more than the last comparable creek front sale in all of Southwest Missouri?"

"So, who is this buyer of yours?"

"I can only reveal his name to a potentially serious seller."

"Well, I'm not one of those. This place was priceless when it came our way, and it will remain that way as long as I'm alive. I suppose I'll get to meet him at some point, anyway. Nope, please thank him or her for their interest, but our farm is not for sale under any circumstances."

"Don't be so sure, sonny boy," the fat man muttered under his breath as he turned and walked away.

Several months later, Heni and Henry got the surprise of their lives, ones that had had more than their fair share of shocks.

Henry was immediately on the phone to his friend Jaime Smith. "Tell me this can't be true, Jaime. The Department of Natural Resources for the state of Missouri has evidently permitted a 6,500-pig confined animal feeding operation for some company named, of all things, Porker Pride. On the old Adams farm, which runs alongside Crane Creek, just upstream from our place. This can't be true, Jaime. Some guy came by to see me not long ago about buying our farm and mentioned his client had acquired the Adams spread for an astronomical price. I had no idea this was in the works and only heard about it at the gas station this morning."

"It gets worse, Henry. No one did. I just found out about it and did a little online research. Any idea who owns Porker Pride, Henry?"

Not waiting for an answer, Jaime proceeded to describe it as a shell company, a limited liability company, to be precise—90 percent owned by XZY, one of the largest meat producers in the world, headquartered in South America, with the remaining 10 percent in private investor hands.

"What does limited liability company mean, Jaime?"

"Just what it sounds like. If anything goes wrong with the operation, the buck stops there, not with the international conglomerate which owns it. It's the way large companies protect their shareholders."

"What? How did this happen without us hearing about it until it's a done deal?"

"Permit applicants are evidently required to post a notice in a local paper and invite comment at a public meeting. These guys chose the *Springfield Gazette*, which no one reads anymore and set the meeting for 7:00 a.m. on a Monday morning at a typically crowded restaurant. Who would ever show up then and there? I had to search exhaustively to even find the notice."

"So, what can we do? We've got to do something?"

"I'm told that we can appeal the permit with the Missouri Clean Water Commission, which, of course, is stacked with agricultural interests. I guess the only other alternative is to go to court. But I'm sure these guys with all of their lawyers and lobbyists followed all the rules. It's just that there aren't many in our state, which has aggressively set out to attract large corporate ag investors, in the purported interest of creating jobs and serving local markets more efficiently."

"We've got to try, Jaime. Let's at least get organized. Can you gather townsfolk for a meeting if I bring in my rural neighbors? I'm wondering, too, whether it makes sense to enlist an attorney to help us."

"Who?"

"Lauren McCall, a lawyer from St. Louis, did an excellent job of making state water law understandable and applicable to our specific situation regarding the Clear Creek Elixir, though it didn't do us much good in the end. In fact, as she described it to us, these bastards are clearly breaking the law."

"Sounds expensive."

"I don't know, but I can approach the Clear Creek Elixir Project leader, Robert Winchell, who is also the editor of the regional magazine Heni still freelances for, to put us in touch. And we can get her freelancing for us immediately in terms of getting the story of this travesty out."

"You just turned a whole lot of dials at one time, Henry. Where and when do we start?"

"Let me find out more about the attorney, and get back to you. In the meantime, start testing the idea of a public meeting on your friends and neighbors. An organizational meeting of sorts. We have got to move quickly. I'm sure Porker Pride is doing exactly that. Back soon."

They were gathered in the local movie theater. There must have been fifty or more standing, sitting, milling around. The background chatter was audible.

Henry strode to the front of the hall and stepped up on a chair. He was accompanied by a well-dressed, middle-aged woman. He whistled to get everyone's attention.

"Thank you for coming tonight. I guess all of you have heard by now about a state-permitted confined animal feeding operation, a CAFO, next to Crane Creek, just upstream from our farm. Does everyone know what a CAFO is? In this case, it is 6,500 pigs crammed snout to curly tail in open-air containment houses and stinking to high heaven. I have been told that such can produce as much putrid waste as a community of 30,000 people, and we treat ours. This is what they are proposing to place next to our precious Crane Creek. We have got to stop it. It will destroy all parts of our community from real estate values to air and water quality and local health. Anybody out there have asthma? Emphysema? COPD? Well, get ready, because this will definitely take your breath away if they get away with it."

Angry murmurs filled the hall. "What can we do, Henry?"

"We need to organize a group to protest this travesty. I say we call ourselves Crane Creek Protectors. I believe we can appeal the permit to the Missouri Clean Water Commission and, failing there, take the matter into the court system. Which is why I have asked the pretty young lady next to me to join us tonight. Let me introduce Lauren McCall, a St. Louis attorney whom I've worked with before on matters of Missouri water law. Ms. McCall can help guide our opposition wherever it takes us and, more importantly, has offered her services pro bono. That means free, folks. Ms. McCall, please," Henry said, pulling up a chair for her to stand on next to him, no easy task given the professional but tight-fitting business suit that adorned her.

Scattered applause broke out. "Why are you helping us for free, Ms. McCall?" A deep voice thundered from the back of the room. "What is in it for you?"

"Just trying to do the right thing, sir. Corporate agriculture and their lobbyists have taken over the statehouse, eliminating or dramatically reducing protections of our water and air, and we have to fight them. This is a fight I am emotionally and morally invested in."

By the time the meeting was over, there was a worked-up mob of locals ready to take on the corporate ag world.

chapter forty-eight

CANE CREEK PROTECTORS

"**G**OOD MORNING, MADAME CHAIR, FELLOW COMMISSIONERS. MY NAME IS LAUREN McCall, and I am representing the citizens group Crane Creek Protectors, a number of whose members have joined me today. We are here as concerned citizens to ask you to revoke the permit for a 6,500-pig CAFO, granted by the Missouri Department of Resources to a shell corporation registered as Porker Pride but majority owned by XZY International, one of the largest pork processors in the world."

"Please proceed, Ms. McCall."

"We object principally to the location of the proposed CAFO next to pristine Crane Creek, which runs through our like-named village in far Southwest Missouri. For those of you who don't know, Crane Creek is home to the rare McCloud trout, which naturally reproduces in its chilly waters, as well as a variety of other unusual animal species.

"As I am sure you are aware, concentrated animal waste is particularly damaging in the Ozarks, where rain, runoff, and seepage through shallow soils represent a clear and present danger to the unique Ozarks karst topography of springs, creeks, streams, lakes, and water tables."

Henry cringed as he observed the inattentiveness of most commission members. From left to right he counted five white males, all with reported affiliations to agricultural interests, from the Farm Bureau to the state senate, and the female chair, also an owner of a cattle farm. One commissioner was absent. All had been appointed by a two-term Republican governor to replace less compliant commissioners. This did not have a fair feel about it.

In actual fact, Henry was not surprised because he had read of the state's renewed interest in expanding its corporate agriculture base. As other Midwestern states had tightened regulations because of deteriorating water and air quality, Missouri had eliminated most of its, including local control through health commissions and zoning restrictions as applied to CAFOs. "Jobs, jobs, jobs" was what proponents shouted to legislators, as they greased palms along the way. It was just stunning to see it so up close and personal.

"We are also concerned," Lauren continued, "that the permittee is not even an adequately capitalized entity and, as a limited liability company, cannot guaranty access to its owner's financial resources in the event of any kind of accident or related damage to the surrounding environment. Nor does the promise of economic development carry any credibility beyond four or five low-paying jobs related to feeding the animals and distributing their waste. The operating contract provides that XZY International will supply Porker Pride with pigs, feed, medicine, and build/lease confinement facilities to them at a fixed rate. All Porker Pride must do is keep the pigs alive, fatten them for market, and funnel waste into storage lagoons, later to be sprayed as fertilizer on adjoining fields. All of which renders Crane Creek vulnerable to rain-driven runoff, lagoon leakage, or overflow and my clients' real estate values, water table, and breathable air at dire risk. Sixty-five hundred pigs can produce waste equivalent to a town of 30,000 people, and they are required to treat theirs. The location proposed for this pig CAFO is simply absurd, and we ask you to reject it, in the name of clean water and air and small community values."

Boisterous applause erupted from the back of the room, with most standing and clapping.

The commission sat in stony silence. Finally the lady chair spoke into her mic. "The Missouri Clean Water Commission does not set policy. That is the state legislators' responsibility. We are here to assure that CAFO applicants adhere to state regulations as established by the legislature. No more. No less. And in this case, it appears as if Porker Pride has followed all the rules. Their plans abide by prescribed setbacks, both from water and from adjoining properties. Their construction drawings seem appropriate. Their sewage lagoons are built to twenty-five-year floodplain specifications."

"Excuse me, Madame Chair, but how many twenty-five-year events has our state had in the past ten years?" interrupted Lauren McCall.

"May I continue, Ms. McCall?" chastised the chair. "Despite no formal guaranties, their parent company would seem to be financially strong enough to maintain satisfactory operating status. And common sense dictates that XZY International's financial interests will be best served by doing so. Finally, it would seem to me a few jobs will be better than none in a small community like yours. Would any of my fellow commissioners care to add anything?"

An elderly gentlemen raised his hand. "I agree with your conclusions, Madame Chairwoman. I don't even believe we need a formal vote as there seems to be nothing to vote on." Others nodded in agreement up and down the line of bored faces.

"Thanks for attending today, Crane Creek Protectors, and please don't ever hesitate to come and share your opinions or questions. The next agenda item is. . . ."

As the crowd gathered around Lauren McCall in the hall outside the meeting room, sobs, curses, and angry voices filled the initial void of shocked silence.

Lauren McCall raised her hands to quiet the gathering. "This was to be expected, ladies and gentlemen. The state's regulation of corporate farming activities is intentionally minimal. The barn door to industrial farm animal production is propped wide open. This will not change until folks like you vote the bastards out. In the meantime our only remaining recourse, short of guerrilla warfare, is the court system. With your permission, this is where we will head next."

"I say let them build it then blow the whole damn thing up," shouted one irate voice from the back.

"Think of the damage that will do to your precious Crane Creek, sir. No, I have some ideas about how to stop this thing by legal means. See you in court."

chapter forty-nine

YOUR HONOR . . . IF YOU PLEASE

"**Y**OUR HONOR . . . IF YOU PLEASE, I WOULD LIKE TO PRESENT MY FINAL TWO witnesses."

Lauren McCall had huddled with Heni and Henry immediately following the Clean Water Commission fiasco.

"Don't lose hope, and please don't let your citizen colleagues get down. I have a strategy to earn a stay and, ultimately, a cease and desist order against the Porker Pride pig CAFO. The logic is simple . . . and logical."

"Please share," urged Heni.

"Do you remember when I presented Michael's team an abbreviated version of Missouri law as regards water rights?"

"Yes, but not the details."

"Something to do with riparian as I recall," chimed in Henry.

"Very good, Henry. Missouri is a riparian water law state. Creek water belongs to the people of the state, and public use of navigable streams is allowed. The land under a creek, on the other hand, belongs to the landholders adjacent to it, who, in turn, control access to the water from stream bank.

"Riparian translates into all landowners whose property touches or lies above a creek have a right to reasonable use of the water. This includes taking water for use on their property, if reasonable and doesn't deprive other landowners of their riparian rights. This was the legal theory we used to justify Hobert and Ethel's right to withdraw water to boil for Crane Creek Elixir, as well as their right to assign the same to us. We never had to test it in court, but I'm convinced it would have held.

"Porker Pride's architectural plans, as presented to the Missouri DNR, envision pumping water directly from Crane Creek into holding tanks for use in diluting effluent and channeling it into sewage lagoons. Their withdrawal of water from Crane Creek is probably reasonable and allowed but only if it doesn't deprive other landholders, namely you two, of your own riparian rights.

"I will argue that Porker Pride, by withdrawing water from Crane Creek to be used to transition tons of waste into slurry for storage in sewage lagoons and subsequent spraying on adjoining fields, is potentially compromising the quality of your water and depriving you of your riparian rights. Runoff from rain soakings and leaching through karst topography will pollute Crane Creek and the local water table, which is the source of your drinking water."

"Can you say all of that again, Lauren? Very, very slowly?"

She did. Two more times before Heni and Henry got it all.

"It's a bit of a stretch but a logical one from my point of view.

"I am definitely prepared to give it a go!"

"Lauren, you must allow us to compensate you for your time, you are investing so much in this."

"Absolutely not. My compensation will be protecting Crane Creek from the ravages of an industrial piggery."

It took Lauren McCall a month to secure a date to present her case in district court, during which time the containment houses were erected and two lagoons excavated. Porker Pride was almost ready for its first shipment of sows.

Judge Sephus Mooning was known as somewhat of a simple, if consistently conservative, thinker, not unlike his constituents. This did not frighten Lauren in that her case rested on simple logic and was conservative in its strict interpretation of Missouri Riparian Law.

Porker Pride was represented by a local Springfield law firm, with a strong XZY corporate bench riding shotgun.

Lauren McCall's initial presentation did not seem to arouse much interest in the courtroom, beyond heavy eye-rolling from the defendants' table. Judge Mooning listened, took no notes, and simply nodded when she was finished.

The Porker Pride response also rested heavily on their riparian right to withdraw water for use in their operations and return it unaltered to creek source. No damages could be assumed, only proven, after the fact. And since their processes had proven safe and secure in countless other venues, there was no reason to fear for the health of Crane Creek, any more than from Henry Hoary's flock of chickens and milk cow.

"Comparing 6,500 pigs and their excrement to two dozen chickens and an old cow is an insult to all of our collective intelligences, Your Honor," responded McCall.

Judge Mooning nodded in agreement, pounded his gavel, and announced he would study both arguments more closely. In the meantime, he placed a thirty-day stay on CAFO operations, to the disbelief of Porker Pride's cadre of attorneys. They appealed the stay vigorously, but Judge Mooning tired of their histrionics and simply rose and walked out.

It was definitely not a win for Protectors but a welcome delay.

Three weeks later, Judge Mooning called both lead attorneys in for a pretrial briefing. He confessed to having misgivings about both sides' arguments but was leaning toward the "not guilty until proven so" defense of Porker Pride's riparian rights. It did trouble him, as a native Ozarker, that a locale more conducive to corporate farming than a pristine creek bearing rare species had not been selected. If indeed the "guilty . . . was proven so," it would be too late to do anything about it other than seek damages. But his job was to interpret the law, not make it.

He asked in closing that if Ms. McCall had any additional witnesses to proclaim the special nature of Crane Creek and its heightened sensitivity to environmental degradation, she should present them in court the following week, when Judge Mooning had promised a ruling.

Lauren met with Henry, Heni, and Jaime immediately after court was adjourned. She wore a concerned look before blurting out, "I am so sorry, but we need to reveal her to save her."

"Your Honor . . . if you please, I would like to present my final witnesses, the first in absentia."

chapter fifty

MAGIC

"JUDGE MOONING, MY FIRST WITNESS, DR. DOROTHY LEAKE, DIED IN 1990 AT THE AGE of ninety-six years," began Lauren McCall.

"I object, Your Honor!" screamed the lead Porker Pride attorney, standing and waving his fist at Ms. McCall. "How can a dead lady give relevant testimony thirty-four years after the fact?"

"He has a point, Ms. McCall," responded Judge Mooning.

"If Your Honor will simply permit me to read briefly from several of her published works, I believe he will sense the relevance."

"OK. Objection overruled. You may proceed, Ms. McCall."

"This is criminal, Your Honor," spat out the angry defense attorney.

"Unusual but not criminal, Counselor. Now sit down and listen, or I will have no alternative to throwing you out of my courtroom. Ms. McCall?"

Lauren McCall proceeded to provide background information on Dr. Leake. How she had lived at the headwaters of Crane Creek for more than seventy years, both pre- and postretirement. How she was educated at Drury College, the University of Missouri, Columbia University, and received a PhD from the University of Oklahoma. How she became a noted university professor and researcher, focused principally on species of algae native to Ozarkian streams. How she and her husband established a freshwater biology station on their 130 acres at Crane Creek, dedicated to preserving the unique water quality of the stream. How she opened up the station to other educational institutions for student access and study.

McCall then proceeded to share several quotes from Dr. Leake's published scholarly papers regarding Crane Creek's unique pristine nature and the unusual flora and fauna it supported.

"There is so much more I could share, Your Honor, but I hope I have established Dr. Leake as an expert in her field and on Crane Creek, with its unusual and unique attributes."

Judge Mooning simply nodded.

"Please take the witness stand, Doctor. May I introduce Dr. William Thrush, internationally renowned scientist and humanitarian, and a principal consultant to the Clear Creek Elixir Project. My next witness was also a vital contributor to the project."

"I object, Your Honor. We all know that project was discredited as a hoax and get-rich-quick scheme, initially led by an outcast from the international scientific community. What could it possibly have to do with our properly awarded permit to raise pigs and create jobs in an impoverished rural community in Southwest Missouri?"

"Your Honor, as you will recall, our discredited project was the result of an intensive negative public relations campaign initiated by Pharma-Lax, Inc., to assure the financial success of their vaccine. Our product, Clear Creek Elixir, has been vetted and tested extensively and proven to provide both a cure for and protection from the coronavirus. In fact it is still available in several retail outlets with no objections by the FDA. We chose not to sue Pharma-Lax for their malfeasance because their vaccine did indeed work, was saving lives, and would eventually put the coronavirus out of business. Making money was never our objective. A lengthy and expensive lawsuit would have served no purpose beyond revenge and padding attorneys' pockets. Our project was not a hoax, and Dr. Thrush will connect the dots between it and Crane Creek in his testimony. It is with great trepidation and fear of the price of disclosure that I make, and will substantiate, the following statement: Your Honor, Crane Creek has magical qualities and must be protected at all cost."

"You are going to allow us to plunge into the world of magic and fantasy to try and stop our legally approved permit from being protected, Your Honor?"

Judge Mooning looked intrigued. "You may proceed with the witness, Madame Counselor."

Lauren McCall asked Dr. Thrush to begin with a recounting of his long and mutually respectful relationship with Dr. Irving Randall. She then requested that he summarize how Dr. Randall brought him in on his unprecedented discovery that Crane Creek possessed magical curative powers as related to the coronavirus.

Dr. Thrush confirmed their interaction, the studies that followed, and his role in the technical analysis. "These unique powers probably sourced as a rare chemical bonding between particles from a meteor strike interacting with pristine Crane Creek to create 'healing' molecules, which, in fact, cured two known corona sufferers who, near death, simply laid in the creek and recovered immediately. Our project's own Henrietta White, who was one of them, has shared her story universally. I can vouch for her and for the integrity of Dr. Randall's conclusions."

"Enough, Dr. Thrush," interrupted Judge Mooning. "None of us comprehends a word of what you are saying, nor do I understand what bearing all of this has on the case at hand."

"If I may Judge Mooning . . . everything," interjected Ms. McCall. "The waters of Crane Creek are blessed with unique healing powers as relates to the coronavirus and who knows what else. The science behind the reasons is admittedly confusing, but the results are not. My next witness will add clarity.

"Let the record show that Dr. Thrush reviewed Dr. Randall's research on Crane Creek and the coronavirus, concurred with his findings, and stepped in to manage his test lab when Dr. Randall couldn't.

"Dr. Thrush, will you testify under oath that the patients you treated with purified Crane Creek water were all cured?"

"Yes, during my limited time of involvement."

"100 percent?"

"100 percent."

"And further that all frontline medical staff who took the elixir as an immunity booster and who cared for those patients up close and personal did so without protective gear? And not one contracted the virus? Again, under oath."

"Yes."

"And finally, Dr. Thrush, that Clear Creek Elixir is no more than purified Crane Creek water?"

"That is correct, Ms. McCall."

"Can you document how many patients and staff were involved in the test lab overall?"

"I would prefer to defer to Ms. Rachel Roberts, CEO of the hospital group we worked with, to provide exact numbers, if OK?"

"That is fine, Dr. Thrush. She is my next witness. And, incidentally, she is known as Rachel Roberts-Winchell now."

"She and Robert got married?"

"Madame Counselor, next witness, please, unless the defense team has other questions for the good doctor," Judge Mooning interrupted with a smile.

"We still do not see the relevance of any of this, from magic water to surprise marriages, as regards our permit affirmation, Your Honor, and request that you stop this ridiculous waste of time immediately. To raise questions would simply be to waste more of it."

"Next witness, Ms. McCall."

"Mrs. Rachel Roberts-Winchell, will you please take the witness stand and be sworn in?"

"Mrs. Roberts-Winchell, you serve as CEO of one the largest hospital groups in the St. Louis region, is that correct?"

"Yes."

"You were also involved intimately in the Clear Creek Elixir Project and hosted the test lab where, for over a month, Dr. Irving Randall, then Dr. William Finch, tested the elixir on your sickest corona patients, with unprotected medical staff?"

"That is correct, Counselor."

"Can you confirm Dr. Thrush's testimony that you realized nearly a 100 percent cure rate when applying Clear Creek Elixir therapies to your most seriously ill corona patients and suffered no staff infections from caring for these patients without protective gear, after taking the elixir as an immunity booster?"

"Ninety plus percent, for the whole test run, Counselor."

"Can you give us an estimate of how many patients and staff were involved in test lab?"

"I can give you an exact number, as Dr. Randall insisted on maintaining detailed records for all patients and medical staff.

"Such things as age, gender, race, first dates of symptoms showing, hospital admission dates, temperatures, pulse-ox rates, recovery dates, and the like.

"In sum, more than 400 patients were admitted into the lab over a period of a little more than a month. Three hundred eighty patients were cured completely and formally released after one dose of Clear Creek Elixir. A 95 percent success rate. There were no deaths which could solely be attributed to the virus.

"At the same time approximately forty medical staff, including myself, were exposed to infected patients without protective gear over the period, and none became infected.

"Our facility and staff would have simply been overrun without the rapid rate of cure and release."

"Why are these numbers not widely known or shared?" asked Judge Mooning.

"Ask Pharma-Lax, International, Your Honor," replied Lauren.

"Is there still not a need for a cure?"

"Yes, thankfully a diminishing one as the vaccine boosts immunity to the virus around the world. And our cure is still available for those who request it, as we continue to bottle it in small batches."

"So, what are you asking, Madame Counselor?"

"I'm asking the court to stay the Porker Pride CAFO indefinitely in the interest of protecting a state and national treasure, a small but beautiful and curative creek.

"Madame Counselor, your presentation seems to be more about gaining state or national protection for a special creek in Southwest Missouri, which is beyond this court's jurisdiction."

"With your permission, I would like to call just one more witness to speak to that issue directly."

"Your Honor, I object. It is irrelevant to the case at hand. We have suffered through enough tangential and irrelevant testimony today and need to focus on the matter at hand, getting our pig farm up and running, to the benefit of a small community, and all involved."

"Sit down, son. You're not losing any ground, in fact you may be winning. Your witness, Counselor. I assume he or she is here?"

"Yes, Your Honor. I call Mr. Robert Winchell, Editor of the *Midwestern Viewpoint Magazine* to the stand. Mr. Winchell was also the executive director of the Clear Creek Elixir Project and has been working for some time to gain federal protection for Crane Creek. Will you expound on your efforts, Mr. Winchell?"

"For sure. Thank you, Your Honor, for allowing me to barge into the proceedings at this late hour, but it is important that you know I agree totally with your conclusion. Crane Creek should never have been exposed to risks like Porker Pride is exploiting. It should have been protected since the beginning. It is clear the state wants nothing to do with that, so federal protection is the most logical course.

"To do so requires revealing Crane Creek's curative powers and the documentation to confirm them. We were sworn to secrecy by the owners of the property who allowed us access to the water for the Clear Creek Elixir. One of them was cured of the virus by laying in the creek, seventy-five-year-old Ethel Campbell, and both she and her husband feared that exposure of the creek as cure would lead to its abuse and ruin.

"We abdicate that promise today to save, not destroy, their special creek. As Counselor McCall told us, 'We need to reveal her to save her.' And that is what we are doing here and now."

"Gaining federal protection will no doubt take time and political clout, Mr. Winchell."

"Which is what we are appealing to you for, Your Honor. The time to approach close contacts in the White House with a proposal for the president to establish the Crane Creek National Wildlife Refuge per executive order. With pristine waters and rare specie inhabitants, it most certainly should qualify for such protection. The president has that authority and has used it on occasion. And the political clout you, as a conservative Republican judge in a state he very much needs in his column for reelection, lend to us by granting the time to pursue designation."

"Your Honor, forgive me, but they are blowing smoke up your robe while we are sitting on a facility ready to serve the community, the state, and the world."

"How much time are you asking for, Mr. Winchell? I cannot shutter a project ready to open its doors indefinitely."

"If you can give us six months to a year to attain approval for such designation, you will have given us a shot."

"Done. The Porker Pride permit to operate a 6,500-pig CAFO along Crane Creek is stayed until six months from today, at which time we will gather here to assess progress."

"You can't do this, Your Honor. On what grounds do you rule?"

"On the grounds of seeking to protect and preserve a special creek in Southwest Missouri from degradation and ruination, at a minimal inconvenience to you and your deep pockets, sir. Case postponed."

Lauren McCall rushed to the bench alone to thank Judge Mooning for his patience and understanding.

"You understand, Counselor, I will not be able to delay further than the appointed date? Maybe nothing in this case is fair, but putting these boys out of business indefinitely certainly isn't. I do applaud your efforts, however. You presented a strong case for preservation of a unique resource."

"Thank you, Judge Mooning."

"Didn't they do this with some other creek a while back? Think I read a book about it? Skunk Creek or something like that?"

"I think the book was *Swine Branch*, Your Honor, about a Skunk Creek, written by Ms. Randi Philander?"

"Yes, that was it, Counselor. I just hope you don't have to go through all the shenanigans with the president of the United States those poor ladies did," Judge Mooning said with a wink.

"Your Honor, that was fiction."

"Oh? Sure seemed real to me."

chapter fifty-one

A RESTROSPECTIVE

EMMA SAT ON THE HILL BEHIND THE CABIN LOOKING OUT ON PART-TIME LOVER AND full-time maintenance man Charlie as he laid his nude body into Crane Creek's frigid waters. Emma had survived several such relationships in her thirty years, as well as a fairly recent divorce. She had no little ones to show from any of it but remained hopeful the right someone would come along to provide her with the love and impetus to raise a family. She really wasn't picky, male or female, but "just right," like her own folks had been for one another.

Thankfully, Emma favored her mom, Heni, in appearance. Thin, athletic, dark skin, sparking black eyes. She was, as her dad always said, "a knockout." He also had referred to her as "child prodigy," "supernatural," "extrasensory," and "transcendent," among other superlatives along the way. Her daddy had almost worshipped her and generally spoiled her, which she guessed was why she hadn't found the perfect man yet. He had held a particular reverence in his heart about her melding with the natural world. He had loved it when she ripped off her clothes as a preschooler, jumped into Crane Creek, paddled around underwater, and surfaced with a small McCloud trout in her hand. He had been less enamored of finding her curled up next to one of Crane Creek's monster cottonmouths, stroking its belly lightly, but had developed a strong trust in her innate sensibilities. Growing up alongside Crane Creek with two adoring parents was a gift unlike any other.

She glanced to her left and saw two clusters of two gravestone markers each atop the hill, looking down on the creek. One honored Ethel and Hobart Campbell, the elderly couple from California who had built the cabin, the site selected with a sensitivity to balance and viewpoints across the valley.

The second sadly memorialized Heni and Henry, who had left this life behind at far too early an age. At least they went together as both would have wished it. They fell to their deaths while hiking their favorite terrain, outside the Ozarks, in southern Utah. Heni had slipped off a rocky spine in a little-known state park but managed to cling briefly to a rock extension. Henry had grabbed her hand and tried to set his feet to pull her up but slipped and tumbled with her a couple of hundred feet to a canyon rock bottom below. At least that is how park rangers envisioned it happening when they found them. A canyon hiker had heard their cries and looked up in horror to see them hurtling to their deaths, hand in hand, as best he could tell. He alerted authorities as soon as he could make cell phone contact. Foul play was never even a consideration. It was simply accidental death on impact.

Emma had been twenty-seven at the time and recently married. She couldn't shake off her loss, and neither could the marriage. She returned to the cabin and had lived there since, with their memory and the critters she had grown up with. Her two brothers, Hank and Harry, who lived on either coast, helped her arrange for their cremation wishes and gravestones to serve as historical markers, looking out over the creek that had been their life. They read:

"Henrietta (Heni) White Hoary, born March 21, 1990, wed July 7, 2022, died September 21, 2048, together as always."

"Henry James Hoary, born October 30, 1990, wed July 7, 2022, died September 21, 2048, together as always."

Both sets of ashes had been distributed by the handful down the hill and into the creek. Emma missed them profoundly.

Crane Creek itself runs as clear and pristine as it always has, under federal protection as the Crane Creek National Wildlife Refuge. It was created by executive order in the spring of 2025 and is administered by the US Fish and Wildlife Service. It is one of many national wildlife refuges that have been established in every state in the union.

Emma had learned over the years that its designation had protected Crane Creek from a large confined animal feeding operation and that her parents were among the local leaders who had fought to get it. They didn't talk about it much, but their love of creek spoke to its import. It became a major source of pride to Emma and her brothers the more they learned of their parents' shared activism.

Emma and the boys were awed by the stories of the times when Heni and Henry got together. Their coronalove, as they called it, was forged in the crucible of a global pandemic, a rampaging coronavirus, political unrest and corruption, and corporate malfeasance. As they delved deeper as young adults and their folks shared more, the adventures and dangers of growing up in the early 2020s read more as fiction than real life.

Their love was almost at first sight, wearing masks and sheltering in place, ultimately together, they finally admitted. A Black lady from the ghetto and a white boy from the Mozarks were an unlikely couple in Springfield, Missouri, at any time, let alone one of such crisis. The horrid Bible-spouting pervert who had stalked Heni, passed the virus to her by forcibly kissing and spitting into her mouth in a grocery store parking lot, and later kidnapped her was the thing of nightmares. That she was cured by laying in Crane Creek and saved by stabbing her abductor to death in the throat, all the while carrying Emma in her belly, spoke to a strong woman.

And their efforts to bring a prevention and a cure for the virus to the world, boiling and bottling the waters of Crane Creek with Hobart and Ethel's permission, only to have an international conglomerate violently disrupt their project with a physical and character assassination campaign, accentuated by a foreign government's kidnapping of Henry and his unlikely escape in an empty casket not 100 yards from the Crane Creek source of healing that his abductors were trying to ransom him for, left their heads spinning. A premature childbirth and subsequent marriage punctuated a two-year run of unprecedented personal, local, and global chaos.

Emma smiled when she thought back on it. The rest of their time together—Heni, Henry, Emma, Hank, and Harry—had been uneventful in that context. A tight, loving, sharing family raised in a cabin overlooking the most beautiful creek in the world, spending more time outdoors than in, growing, thriving, and pursuing their dreams in alternative fashions. Both brothers were married now, with kids of their own. Emma's marriage was the only one that hadn't worked out, but she had found peace in the valley of the Crane Creek National Wildlife Refuge.

Emma moved past her memories and walked down to the creek. She slowly shed her clothing and joined her friend in the healing waters. Who knows, she thought to herself, maybe he will become my Henry and I his Heni. If so, I wonder what we can call our love. Definitely not corona. . . .

THE END

TODD PARNELL

Todd Parnell is the retired President of Drury University, founding CEO of THE BANK in Springfield, Mo., civic leader, environmental advocate as co-founder of the Upper White River Basin Foundation and retired Chairman of the Missouri Clean Water Commission, and award-winning author inducted into the Missouri Writers Hall of Fame in 2012. He holds Masters degrees in Business Administration from Dartmouth University and History from Missouri State University, and an undergraduate degree from Drury University.

Parnell began writing non-fiction during his years as a banker and educator, including published works *The Buffalo, Ben, and Me, Trails of the Heart: Along the Buffalo River, Mom at War,* and *Postcards from Branson.* He tried his hand at fiction upon retiring from the Drury presidency and hasn't stopped writing since, publishing the Ozarkian Folk Tales Trilogy (*Skunk Creek, Swine Branch,* and *Donny Brook*), and the Children of the Creek Trilogy (*Wellspring of Evil, Stream of Life,* and *Life is a River.*) Recent releases include Pig Farm (2018), a sweeping and rollicking historical tall tale set in the context of a real time environmental tragedy along the Buffalo National River, *Privilege and Privation—A Love Story* (2019), a tale of two young people from diametrically diverse economic backgrounds who fall in love, and *The Posse* (2020), a story of love, and resistance.

Parnell was born in Branson, Mo. and is an eighth-generation Ozarker. He resides with his wife of 44 years, Betty, in Springfield, Mo. and is blessed with four children and five grandchildren. The Parnells were inaugural co-chairs of the Every Child Promise initiative, and served on its executive advisory board.

DR. PATRICK PARNELL

Dr. Patrick Parnell is a retired practicing veterinarian and city councilman from Branson, MO.

He is an eighth-generation Ozarker and currently resides in Batesville, AR with his wife Melissa.

www.ingramcontent.com/pod-product-compliance
Lightning Source LLC
Chambersburg PA
CBHW030529020726
47494CB00004B/1284